THE
HANDS
OF LOVE

OMAR SCOTT

Outskirts Press, Inc.
Denver, Colorado

Outskirts Press, Inc.
http://www.outskirtspress.com

ISBN: 978-1-4327-3402-2

Outskirts Press and the "OP" logo are trademarks belonging to Outskirts Press, Inc.

PRINTED IN THE UNITED STATES OF AMERICA

CHAPTER 1

Lorenzo Love is not your average fifteen year veteran detective. Ren, as he's better known, is a high octane control freak that was born with a chip on his shoulder. He knows the streets like no other- mainly because he was raised in them. He is well connected on the force, and extremely intelligent. That's why he has been put in charge of an experimental narcotic unit called the Ghost Squad. This unit was created to investigate high levels of drug trafficking and gang related activity. Ren and his team use unconventional and sometimes questionable tactics to get results that are expected of them, and this situation was no different. They were about to execute a warrant on the notorious Morris Jones aka Momo. He was the leader of the PG's (Pleasant Grove Gangsters), a gang that runs heroine on the east side of Dallas. A man like Ren, with lots of power and little self control can be very dangerous, and you're about to see just how dangerous.

Ren and his squad pulled up to Momo's

plush home around eight in the morning. The sun had just risen, along with the hot Texas heat. Momo's crib was in an old rundown area, but he had made a lot of upgrades to his place. He wanted a luxurious house, but he wanted to stay close to the neighborhood so that he could keep his eye on business. Therefore, he spent big dollars to get his home up to his standards. The landscaping was immaculate. He had a pool with a waterfall and a large gazebo built in the backyard that was secluded with an eight-foot high privacy fence. He had high dollar window treatments and siding added to the exterior of his home to make it look new again. The inside of the house had also been totally redone. Hardwood floors were placed throughout the house. Crown molding and hand carved paneling decorated the walls. He installed Moen faucets, remote controlled ceiling fans, and a custom stone fireplace which added an exquisite touch to the house. Momo had put thousands into making his home his personal oasis.

Slamming the car door, Ren surveyed the scene as he walked toward the back of his vehicle. Gazing at the sun for a second, Ren's butterscotch looking eyes sparkled under the bright sunlight. The street was empty for the most part. School bells had already rung, and Ren had noticed the crossing guard at the end of the block was getting in his car to leave. Searching for the right key, Ren opened the trunk and handed all the members of the Ghost

Squad bulletproof vests. Grabbing a twelve-gauge shotgun as well, he slammed the trunk closed. He took a stick of gum out of his pocket, popped it into his mouth, and turned to his guys. With the sun on his back, his muscular build cast a shadow over the men of his unit as he addressed them in his smooth voice. "Alright listen up boys. Manny, you and Keith cover the rear entrance. Jason, you hit the front door with me, and Dwayne you're backup. Switch to channel five on your radios. Everybody got it?"

"Got it!" the guys replied, heading to take their positions.

Jason followed Ren, as he lumbered over to the front door with a heavy metal battering-ram he was carrying. Ren dropped to one knee, and gently jiggled the doorknob just to make sure that it wasn't unlocked before they hit it. He turned to the backup man Dwayne, and gave him a thumbs-up.

"Are you good to go?" Dwayne asked talking into his radio.

"Ten-four. We're good to go." Manny shot back, from their position in the rear of the house.

Dwayne pulled out his nine millimeter and nodded his head to Ren. Jason started to swing the ram, then, Bam! The door flew open as they rushed in with their heads on a swivel. It was early Friday morning and Momo was still dressed in his robe with his hair uncombed. Relaxing on his plush leather couch in the living room, Momo was watching *Good Morning*

America while eating a bowl of Raisin Bran. Calmly, Momo sat up on the couch, put his bowl down, and made no quick moves. Not even to grab the .38 revolver sitting on the coffee table in front of him.

"Freeze! Don't move!" Ren commanded.

Manny and Keith kicked in the back door simultaneously. Once they secured the kitchen, they searched the additional rooms to make sure that nobody else was in the house.

Jason stood there with his shotgun aimed at Momo's head while Ren walked over and casually sat down in the armchair across from him. He pulled out his radio. "Area secured," he said to Dwayne, who was still outside.

"How are you doing, Momo?" Ren asked with a smile on his face as he kicked up his Nike's on the coffee table.

"Well, well, well, if it isn't Lorenzo Love and the Ghost Squad my favorite set of cops," Momo replied looking down at Ren's feet on his coffee table. "Do you mind? That's Ethan Allen. I spent a grand on that table. And by the way, you didn't have to kick in my doors. All you had to do was knock; I would have voluntarily opened it."

"Momo, I don't think it matters much, a broken door is the least of your problems."

"I know," Momo replied shaking his head.

"You fucked up. You fucked up big time Mo, but I have a way out for you. Unfortunately it's going to require you going to jail,"

THE HANDS OF LOVE · 5

Ren proclaimed locking eyes with Momo.

"What the hell are you talking about Ren?"

"I'm talking about a dead cop, and a city out for blood. Didn't you hear the police chief's speech? You're *Public Enemy Number One* my man," Ren stated while he grabbed some peanuts out of a jar that was on the table, and stuffed them in his mouth.

"It had to be done Ren. He was getting too close to us. He could've brought us all down. Don't get mad at me for having the balls to take care of business. Remember we still have a deal," Momo said pointing at Ren.

"That deal was predicated on the fact that there would be no violence. Not only was there violence, but you killed a fucking undercover cop. That's a deal breaker Mo," Ren said sarcastically.

"So what kinda trumped up charge you trying to pin on me?"

"Possession with intent to deliver, what else?"

"How are you going to prove it? I haven't been close to any dope."

"Yes you have." Ren looked up and gestured to Keith. Keith ran back to the car, and reappeared with a large duffle bag. Opening up the bag, he pulled out a clear plastic bag that was full of smaller bags of heroine. Without a word, he walked over and set the bag on the table next to Momo.

Momo's stoic look never changed. He was

known to be calm under pressure. You'd have to be to run a drug organization that was as big as his. Momo's crew controlled the ntire Pleasant Grove section of Dallas. He ruled with an iron fist, despite his small stature and good looks. Only five-foot seven, his small hundred and sixty pound frame was hardly intimidating. But nobody dared messed with him. His reputation spoke for itself. Once, he beat a man to death with his bare hands for calling his lady a bitch. You see, Momo was the ultimate gentleman. He never cursed. He always opened doors and pulled out chairs for ladies. He would never, under any circumstances, allow a woman to be mistreated or disrespected.

"What's that?"

"It's your drugs."

"You gotta be kidding," Momo joked with a slight chuckle.

"Oh, I'm afraid not, Mo. You can't kill a cop in this city and expect a free pass. You got an entire police force on your back right now that wants to crucify your ass. You're lucky I'm here instead of them, or you'd have a bullet in your head right now."

"I know, I know," Momo replied looking down at the floor.

"Relax; be glad you're not being charged with first-degree murder. Drug possession charges like this, you'll do five years max. That's enough time to let the dust settle. The public can feel safe that a cop killer is off the streets. The brass can break their arms patting themselves on the back for the job they've done. And maybe, just maybe I'll get the promotion I've been waiting for," Ren stated with a slight grin. "By the way, there's also one more matter."

"Yeah? What's that?"

"A little matter of my fee for straightening up this whole situation for you. So, where's your stash at?"

"What stash?" Momo snapped.

"Don't play dumb. I know you keep it here."

"Oh! So on top of charging me with some bogus shit, you motherfuckas are gonna jack me too? This is bullshit!"

"Whoa! Momo the gentleman is cursing and losing his temper, I don't believe it."

"Believe it motherfucker! I ain't taking this shit lying down."

"Yes you will."

Dwayne stepped up from behind him and pushed the barrel of his gun against the back of Momo's head. He looked a little nervous, but managed to keep his hands steady. Jason also stepped closer and put that gauge only inches from Momo's forehead.

"Now at the end of the day, my boss really doesn't care whether I bring your ass in dead or alive. But I like you Mo, so I'm gonna give you one more chance. But don't test my patience. So, for the last time, where is the money?"

Momo knew he was in between a rock and a

hard place. He swallowed his pride and pointed to the picture on the wall. Keith ran over and threw down the picture to reveal a safe.

"Combination please," Ren said sarcastically getting out of the chair, and walking over to the safe.

Momo was mute for a moment. Then Dwayne pushed him in the back of the head with the gun once again.

"Twelve right, five left, nine right," Momo said, shaking his head in frustration.

Keith opened up the safe and began to thumb through the money. He was the math wiz of the bunch. He majored in accounting when he went to Louisiana State University. It was only in his junior year that he decided to go into criminal justice.

"How much are we looking at Keith?" Ren asked, walking back over to Momo.

He swallowed like he just had a drink of water. "Rough estimate, about five hundred thousand," Keith replied, counting a stack of bills, and then putting the money into the duffle bag that previously held the drugs.

"Well boys, looks like we hit the mother lode." All the guys started smiling at each other and giving high fives.

"Crooked ass cops. I should've never gotten involved with y'all. Y'all got no code. Y'all respect nothing. How do y'all live with yourselves?"

"How do I live with myself? Easy! I'm a

cop doing a public service. You see, Momo, we can't *stop* all crime, but we can *control* it. That's where you come in. You're my bitch. And like a good bitch, as long as you do what you're told, you can operate. The moment you get outta line, is the moment you get smacked like a bitch. And the cash- that's for services rendered." Ren flashed another grin as he sat back down in his armchair. "Now, Manny read this fucker his rights."

Manny walked up behind Momo pulling out the cuffs. "You got the right to remain silent. If you give up the right to remain silent, anything you say can and will be held against you in a court of law. You…"

"Save your breath! I've heard all that crap before. You know this ain't over, right? I ain't going out like this. If I go down, everybody goes down," Momo warned in disgust.

"You know, Momo, I wish you hadn't said that." Ren declared, standing back on his feet.

"Do you know what happens to bitches you can't control?"

"No! What?"

"Keith, what's the name of that Stephen King movie I like? You know the one about the dog?" Ren said snapping his fingers trying to recall it.

"You mean *Cujo*."

"Yeah! Yeah! *Cujo*. You ever saw that Mo?"

"No!"

"You never read the book or saw the movie *Cujo*? See, that's the problem with you youngsters today. Great movie- even better book. Basically, it's a story about a dog that goes crazy. He gets rabies or is possessed by the devil or something, and once the dog was infected he turned on the family. He tried to kill'em all. There were signs in the beginning, when he first snapped at them, that they couldn't trust him no more. But they ignored it. They allowed the shit to go on and on. But you know what I would've done?" Ren asked, staring straight into Momo's eyes.

Momo was still fuming. He hunched his shoulders to acknowledge Ren's question.

"I'd put that motherfucker down the first time he raised up at me."

Ren reached back in his holster and pulled out his 9mm Beretta. Slowly, he aimed at Momo's chest. *Now* he had Momo's full attention as Momo slightly quivered in fear.

"You can't kill me, you're a cop! I thought you said you'd give me a break."

"I lied," Ren admitted squeezing the trigger at point blank range. The bullet pierced Momo's chest with such force that his head snapped back. Momo had a stunned look on his face. His mouth was wide open as he sat there struggling to breathe. Then, blood started gushing out of his chest like a can of soda that had been poked with a knife. His eyes froze wide open while he slid down the couch and slumped over.

CHAPTER 2

The Ship, what the officers called the twelfth precinct building, was a-buzz with activity. They called it The Ship because it was an old rundown car dealership that closed years ago. When the city needed to expand the police department to have a presence in the Pleasant Grove section of Dallas, the city purchased the rundown building and converted it to a station. They didn't put a lot of money into it, just enough to make it functional. When you walked in you could see the high ceilings and fluorescent lights. You could hear the collective sound of fingers hitting their key pads, as cops were typing up reports and prisoners handcuffed to desks being asked questions about their suspected crimes. The sound of coffee being poured into cups and the shuffling of papers filled the air. This Monday morning was a bit different than others. The news of the death of Momo was spreading throughout The Ship like a virus.

Ren and his team walked in The Ship with

their heads high and were greeted with cheers and claps. Ren smiled and bowed like an actor on *Broadway* taking his final *curtain-call.* He probably could've been mistaken for an actor as well. With his clean-shaven face, dark brown skin that was smooth like silk, and soft black wavy hair, he had the looks to make any woman stand up and take notice. His thin lips accentuated his sexy smile, and his magnificent physique was carefully sculpted working out in the officer's weight room daily. He was dressed in his customary blue jeans and t-shirt. Accepting the endless handshakes and pats on the back, he made his way through the lobby.

The Captain came out of his office and announced, "Time for roll call ladies and gentlemen!"

Ren turned around and followed everyone else, as they made their way into the meeting room. The meeting room had a classroom type setting. The officers took their seats as the Captain's assistant was handing out the packets. Marvin Riley, the Captain, stood up in front of the room. He was an older man, who was short, wrinkled, and had bushy eyebrows. Taking the podium he addressed the troops with his raspy voice. "First of all, everybody give it up for the Ghost Squad and the excellent work they did on the Jones case."

Everybody once again started clapping, whistling, and giving them a standing ovation. The Ship had been a place of enormous tension for the last month. When Detective Kevin Benson was murdered in the line of duty it hit the precinct hard. He was only twenty-eight when he was gunned down. Benson, a handsome young black man with a promising career, had just made detective after seven years on the force. He was working his first undercover assignment as a detective, the Jones case, when he was killed.

"Okay you guys settle down. We don't need these boy's egos getting anymore inflated than they are already. Now in front of you, you'll find packets of our new watch list. We got reviews coming up next Monday, so get all your paperwork in order and clear as many files as possible. Also, we've had a rash of burglaries lately. The M.O. on the perps is they use a crowbar to rip open the rear doors of houses in broad daylight. So keep your eyes open on that. That's all I got," the Captain said as the room began to clear instantly.

"Hey Ren, I need to see you in my office for a minute," the Captain blurted out from across the room.

"Okay boss."

Ren followed the Captain into his office and had a seat. His office was that of a typical police captain. His desk was piled high full of file folders, and the walls were packed with pictures of wanted felons. You could barely see his desk. Captain Riley called it an *organized mess.*

Ren and Captain Riley got along well. The

Captain was Ren's first C.O. when he joined the force almost twenty years ago. He helped guide Ren's career carefully. With his backing, Ren became one of the fastest beat cops to ever make detective. The Captain brought him along when he took over command of The Ship. He even made him head of his own experimental narcotics unit, the Ghost Squad.

"So what's up, Captain?" Ren asked casually taking a seat.

"Love, I just wanna say you guys did great work closing that case so fast. The department really needed this. The chief thanks you personally. You and your unit are going to get commendations for this."

"That's fucking great news Captain!"

"That's not all. I got the new lieutenants list. Your name is on it. Your promotion came through," Captain Riley said smiling.

"Don't fuck with me like that Captain. You know I've been waiting on that a long time," Ren said sitting on the edge of his seat.

"I wouldn't do that to you. It won't be official for another month, but congratulations Lieutenant Love," Captain Riley stated as he stood up and firmly shook Ren's hand. "Now look Love, your unit has done well. The chief is pleased. It looks like he has approved the financing to keep the Ghost Squad going permanently. So fill your guys in on the good news."

Riley walked back around his desk and took a seat. A blank look took over his face. "Love as you know Momo had a lot juice in this town. Internal Affairs is going to be watching this situation closely. So I've got to ask you one last time, was everything by the book on this one?"

"Yes sir. We were wearing vest that were clearly marked *police*. We kicked in the door and identified ourselves. He opened fired and we returned fire. Pretty cut and dry, just as it is in my report."

"Good!"

Ren left Riley's office and headed to the club house, that's what he called the Ghost Squad's personal meeting room. It kind of puts you in mind of a high school football locker room. They had a small stereo and TV that they kept on constantly. The TV was usually on ESPN and the radio tuned to *Tom Joyner's Morning Show*. Each guy had their own locker for their personal property. The walls were decorated with an assortment of women's pictures from such magazines like Maxim and Smooth. There was a large table in the middle of the room that they used for not only meetings, but also for such past times as dominoes and cards. The room smelled of tobacco and gun oil. They allowed no one outside the Ghost Squad to enter, except for the Captain.

Ren walked in to see Keith fixing himself a cup of coffee. Keith Sanders was a short, dark-skin, black man with a pencil thin mustache, and a college cut. He and Ren had been best friends since the third grade. They both grew up in the tough Pleasant Grove section of Dallas, where today, they now fight crime in those same streets. They graduated together from the same college; LSU, then Keith followed Ren into law enforcement. Keith's character was in direct contrast to Ren's. He is a reserved, soft spoken, meek individual. The kind of qualities that don't make for a good cop, but since Ren's career really took off, Keith just hopped on his coat-tail and road it to making detective.

Dwayne was filing some paperwork at the table. He was the big man of the crew, the enforcer. When it was time to make the Ghost Squad's presence known Dwayne was front and center. A former linebacker in college for TCU, he never lost his football playing build. Bench pressing over four hundred pounds, he was still incredibly strong. With a deep baritone voice like Barry White, Dwayne always breathed heavily even when he did the most minuet things. He wore a thick goatee on a face that only a mother could love. But that rough and rugged appearance of his was perfect for intimidating criminals on the street.

Sitting on the couch breaking down and cleaning his gun was Jason. He was the only white boy on the crew. It's hard for a white boy to get assigned to The Ship as a detective. Pleasant Grove is a majority black and Hispanic area, and nobody trust white guys. It's hard for them to go undercover, and it's tough to get informants and gang Intel. But despite his blonde hair and blue eyes, Jason was the exception to that rule. His skills on a computer are second to none. Jason could bypass any firewall or hack into any system in the blink of an eye. You're probably wondering why a guy with that kind of skill would be a policeman. Simple. When he was in high school someone went online and stole his father's identity. Then they wiped out his 401k worth a hundred and fifty grand. Thirty years of saving as a factory worker for a freight company. Jason's father, a simple man, didn't know his money was federally insured. His father put a bullet in his head when he heard the news. Jason was the one that discovered the body. It was then and there that he decided he would use his skills to try to find the man responsible.

Manny was looking into a mirror on the wall licking his fingers to make his eyebrows lay down. More playboy than cop at times, he probably spends more time looking at a mirror and combing his hair, than he does working at his desk. He swears up and down that he looks like Marc Anthony the singer. Manny does have one undeniable specialty, his connections. His outgoing and flamboyant personality allows him to have relationships with a variety of different people including the criminal low life.

"Hey boys listen up! I got great news!"

They all dropped what they were doing and huddle up around Ren, except for Manny, who couldn't seem to pull himself away from the mirror.

"Excuse me Manny, I don't mean to break up this love fest between you and yourself, but could you join the rest of us?"

The rest of the guys broke out in laughter as Manny finally made his way over. "Fuck you guys! Don't hate me 'cause I look good," he said straightening out the collar on his Sean-John suit.

"Okay ladies settle down! I just talked to the Captain. He informs me that we're all getting commendations for the Jones case."

"Hell yeah!" All the guys yelled out as they high five each other in celebration. Keith, on the other hand, was silent. Twiddling his thumbs, he had a look on his face like a fifty-year old man that couldn't take a piss at night because of a swollen prostate. Leaning over he whispered into Ren's ear while the rest of the guys were celebrating, "Ren, I really need to talk to you man."

"Sure. You can hit the streets with me. We can go get some lunch," Ren whispered back to Keith, and then he turned back to address the other guys again. "Hey boys, let's celebrate to-night at Johnny's around ten. The first round is on me, but now it's time to hit the streets. Since Momo is out the picture, there's going to be a new soldier vying for the crown. It can only be one of two people, either Tony B or Momo's little brother Red. So Jason, I want you to get started pulling both guys' jackets. I want to know where they live, where they kick it, and who they hang with. Dwayne, Manny, I need you two to over to PG territory. Lean on the soldiers, and see if you guys can get some indication of which way the wind is blowing. Keith and I are gonna pay a visit to our friend Torch. Make sure that South Siders don't try to take advantage of the regime change."

Ren's brief meeting broke up. Keith and him hopped into his car and sped off to get some lunch before hitting the streets. They decided to go by Big Bob's Barbecue on Buckner. Barbecue was one of Ren's favorite foods. He'd eat it every day if he could.

They walked in Bob's and went to the counter to order. It was early in the afternoon, so the place was pretty empty. Bob's had that *greasy-spoon* feel to it. The restaurant was old and decrepit. The ceiling looked like it was made with asbestos and could cave in at any moment. The oven, burners, and heating elements were rusty and out dated. The tables looked like they had been transplanted from the seventies. A young teenage boy walked up with a pad and pen to take their order.

"Can I take your order?" The kid said dryly.

"Yeah, give me a rib lunch plate, and for my friend…"

"Make mines a hot link basket," Keith uttered.

"That'll be thirteen fifty."

"We get the policeman's discount right?" Ren asked as he opened his wallet, and flashed his badge.

The kid squinted his eyes and frowned up his face at that piece of news. He hit a key on the register that dropped their bill down twenty percent. When Ren reached into his wallet and paid him, he noticed that kid's demeanor quickly changed after telling him he was a cop. Ren sees that type of reaction from young black kids from time to time. The kid heads to the back and started to make their plate. Ren was suspicious, so while Keith took his seat at one of the booths and waited for his food, Ren cracked the metal door leading to the kitchen and watched the kid prepare their food. The kid washed his hands and put on some plastic gloves to make the food. Slicing up the meat, he fixed the plates nicely and then when he was done, he spit on their beans and potato salad. Ren just smiled as he was checking this out from behind the metal doors. He quickly closed the cracked door and stood back behind the counter like he had been waiting there the entire time.

"Your orders are ready!" The kid yelled out as he sat their trays on the front counter. Keith walked up to get his plate when Ren stopped him.

"Say kid there's something wrong with these plates," Ren commented grabbing his plate and looking at it from every angle. Picking up a fork, he pretended to poke and prod the food as if he was really looking for something.

"Wrong...what is it?" The kid asked with his eyebrows scrunched together.

"There's something that don't look right about this potato salad."

The kid walked over and looked at both plates carefully, "I don't see anything wrong."

"Come here, look a little bit closer," Ren commanded. The Kid got even closer as he stared down to get a better look. Then without warning, Ren grabbed the back of his neck and slammed his face into the tray.

"You thought it would be cute to spit in my food, huh you little punk!" Ren asked the rhetorical question still holding the kids face down in the potato salad. The kid was struggling to get loose, but Ren was too strong.

"Next time I catch you spitting in mine or anybody else's food, I'm gonna kick your little black ass till I smell shit! Understand?"

"Yes sir! Yes sir!" The kid mumbled with a mouth full of potato salad.

Then Ren slowly let him up. Hearing the commotion, Bob the restaurant owner, came from around back. An older man who just had hip surgery, Bob gingerly made his way to the front counter.

"Everything okay out there Junior?" Bob asked making his way up to the front counter. Bob just came in from outside with a handful of hickory wood to refill the pit when he heard the turmoil.

"Everything's fine Bob. Junior here had a

slight mishap with one of our trays. Ain't that right, Junior?" Ren interjected. The kid standing there with a stupid look on his face covered in potato salad nodded in agreement. Ren pretended to wipe food from the kid's shirt.

"Junior go get cleaned up! I'm sorry officer Love. I'll make you another plate."

The old man got busy in the back, and in no time at all Keith and Ren had two fresh, spit free plates of barbecue. They sat down at the table and began to eat. You could hear the two smacking on the tender beef covered in sauce, as they licked their fingers in between bites. The kid stepped out the washroom with a clean face rolling his eyes at the two. Ren paid him no mind as he focused his attention back to Keith.

"So you said you wanted to talk. What's on your mind?"

"Ren, ah…. I just don't know. I don't feel right about this whole Momo thing," Keith admitted while rubbing his pencil thin mustache. Whenever Keith got nervous, he had the bad habit of rubbing his mustache.

"What's there to know? Momo was a drug dealer that sold smack to kids. He got what he deserved," Ren replied coldly.

"C'mon Ren! It's not that simple. We're cops for Christ's sake."

"Where is all of this concern coming from Keith? It's not like we ain't done this before."

"Yeah, we've taken a few dollars off the books and created a little evidence when it wasn't there to get the conviction. But this is different. We murdered a man."

"Correction," Ren interjected, "We killed a drug dealer and cop killer. Do me a favor, look out that window and tell me what you see?"

Keith looked through the old window. The street was alive with activity. Cars were zooming up the boulevard; a homeless man was pushing a rusty old shopping-cart full of cans down the sidewalk. The Muslims were selling bean-pies and papers at the stop light. Young kids putting fliers for night clubs in the windshields of parked cars. Upon taking in the whole scene, Keith turned around and shrugged his shoulders at Ren.

"Let me tell you what I see," Ren said breaking the silence. "I see a once great neighborhood that the black community could be proud of turned into poverty and despair because of drugs. I also see a police force that is powerless to stop it. I see the good, hardworking, law-abiding people living in fear, scared to let their kids play outside. So, when somebody brings up the rights of some asshole like Momo, I say what about the rights of the families he's hurt. What about the countless lives that Momo destroyed by pushing that smack out there? Huh? What about the justice for those families. Every day that a bastard like Momo walked around free peddling his dope, is a day that justice is denied to those families. Do I have to quote your favorite poet Langston

Hughes to you, "Justice delayed is justice denied". I can't stop these punks from selling dope. But I can control it. Keep that crap out of decent neighborhoods. And at the end of the day, if an opportunity presents itself, I will get a little justice for those families."

"Yeah, but what if we get caught?"

"Relax," Ren replied tilting his head back and looking at the ceiling. "C'mon man, you've known me since we were in the third grade. I was the best man at your wedding. I've been having your back since way back then. I ain't gonna let nothing happen to you. Besides, the whole city wanted that asshole to go down. Nobody is thinking twice about him. Trust me!"

"But ah…"

"Relax. You worry too much. Look, I didn't want to say anything in front of the rest of the guys 'cause it's not official yet, but I'm being promoted to lieutenant. Which means you'll make first grade detective."

"For real?"

"Hell yeah! So stop sweating that shit. Only thing you got to worry about is how you're gonna spend the cash you got."

"What good is the money if we can't spend it anyway?"

"Like I told you guys, only for now. We got to let everything calm down first. Let the dust settle. Trust me. I got everything covered."

"Alright," Keith said feeling a little more reassured.

"Good, now on to something more important. How is that wife of yours?"

"She's doing good. She's eight months now.
We had one of those sonograms the other day."

"Really! So what's it gonna be huh?"

"Doctor said it's gonna be girl."

"That's beautiful man."

"Yeah! We'll have a boy and a girl, and
that's it. Natalie's having her tubes tied after
this. She brought up me getting a vasectomy,
but I told her no way I'm letting a knife get
anywhere close to the family jewels."

"I feel you on that. I wouldn't want a doctor
putting a scalpel to my balls either," Ren said
polishing off the last bit of his food. "I'm gonna
run you back to The Ship and we'll meet up at
Johnny's tonight. Be prepared to have some
drinks and let your dick hang, and that's an order."

CHAPTER 3

Nina had finally finished running her bath water and was ready to get off her dog tired feet. She took off her clothes and started making her way over to the tub. Her feet were so sore that she walked across the bathroom floor like she was stepping on hot coals. It was the price she paid for choosing style over comfort when buying the cute little shoes she likes. She loves to walk around in her stilettos, even at work, where she's on her feet four out of the eight hours that she's there. Testing the water, she put her toe in to make sure the temperature was just right. She slowly began to lower herself in. After a hard afternoon of cleaning the house from top to bottom, this was just what she needed to relax a little. She was ready for *Calgon* to take her away.

Nina had taken the day off work to implement phase one of her plan, get Ren back. Since the birth of their son Michael ten years ago, their relationship had slowly begun to deteriorate. It was nothing dramatic like knock -out -drag -out fights or screaming matches. They just, as the years went by, stop talking as much. It was like they ran out of words to say to each other. They never had much in common to begin with. Their personalities, likes and dislikes were completely different. Ren was assertive and strong willed, while Nina was passive. She liked to meticulously plan things out, while Ren was more of a *go with the flow kind of guy*. He liked to smoke the occasional cigar, and she can't stand them. She was a stay at home, rent a movie, and sit under a blanket girl. He was a nocturnal, drink shots, and partying in the club guy. You're probably thinking how they got together in the first place, as the old saying goes, opposites attract.

She sat there in the warm water thinking. She couldn't help but to conclude that most of this was her fault. She believed that she didn't give her man the attention that he deserved. Plus, after Michael was born she'd put on a little weight. Stepping on the scale just before getting into the tub, she saw that she weighed one-fifty now. A far cry from when she was twenty-five and she weighed about a buck ten. When she was a size four and her ass was firm. When her breast would sit up like a starving dog that just had a treat waved in its face. When her man would gawk at her instead of those other women on the street. Back before she had a kid and had gotten stretch marks. Even though every man she meets tells her how fine she is, it's not coming from the person she wants to hear it from the most, Ren. She wants to feel sexy again in his eyes. That's the only thing that mattered to her. Nina had made up her mind. She was going to win her man back.

She reminisces on how she and Ren met. She was in her senior year at Tulane University just on the outskirts of New Orleans. Mardi Gras was in full effect. It was the spring of 87'. Nina was in the French Quarters down on Bourbon Street, hanging with her girls. It was one of the rare occasions that she let her guards down in public and was getting wasted with her friends. They were sitting at the bar drinking boilermakers and giggling like junior high school girls. That's when she saw him. He walked up with confidence and killer smile. He had a baby face back then that she thought was so cute. He possessed the two most important qualities to her, he was tall and he had long feet, which made her feel confident that he was packing. One of the things that were a must for any man she dated. His smile was sweet like a cold glass of iced tea. The words coming out of his mouth were warm and sincere. The inadvertent way he let his hands touch her shoulders was scintillating. She was mesmerized by Ren's mysterious eyes. The smell of his body was intoxicating. She dug his vibe almost immediately. The conversation, which was magical, was like icing on the cake. As they walked down Bourbon St. looking at the crescent moon they exchanged life stories. Before she knew it, she was sneaking Ren into her dorm room.

The resident director had fallen asleep and they crept passed her to Nina's room which was on the second floor. They quietly slipped into her room where her roommate Stephanie was in her bed fast asleep. The lights in the room were out, but the glow from that crescent moon was peaking through the blinds as they stood over her bed with eyes closed letting their lips meet for the very first time. She could taste the Long Island ice tea that he was drinking earlier as his tongue probed inside her mouth. Slowly unbuttoning her blouse Ren tasted her soft skin that smelled of jasmine. As her blouse fell to the floor his fingers tenderly glided up the small of her back and unhooked her bra to reveal her supple breasts. His touch sent goose bumps up and down her spine. Kneeling down he lightly nibbled on her nipples while unzipping her skirt and allowing it to fall to the floor as well. Ren's strong, warm hands gently squeezed her soft round ass ever so gently. Lifting her up by the waist he placed Nina on the bed and began sucking on her neck like it was a sweet peach. Caressing her firmly to show that he was in total control, his tongue found its way down to her navel and danced inside it. Nina lost control at that point. Her navel was her weak spot, and the slightest stimulation turned her into putty. She immediately lifted her butt off the bed to signify to Ren that it was okay to slide off her panties. Slowly, he removed them as he was face to face with a nicely trimmed pussy that was soaking wet. Letting the tip of his tongue slither over her clit, he licked his way back up her body past her navel and breast to once again meet her soft lips. Rubbing her thighs, he gently pushed her legs up in the air and slowly went in, as the blood pumping into his dick reached its full capacity. With every sensual stroke that Ren delivered, Nina sunk her manicured nails deeper into his ample chest. Pulling him closer to her, she wrapped her legs around his waist and melted into his arms like candle wax. She couldn't contain herself as she screamed out in pleasure. Ren quickly put his hand over her mouth to keep Nina from waking up the entire dorm, but never stopped stroking in the process. Her orgasms were coming back to back. It was at that point when her knees were shaking and she was too weak to move, that she knew she was hooked. There is nothing else in the world that could give her the same bliss, the same intensity, the same exhilarating passion that she got from being in his arms.

Even now, as Nina sat in her jet tub with the water gently massaging her clit, and the thought of that night in her head, was about to bring her to another orgasm. All she needed was the slight touch of her forefinger to bring it out. She wouldn't even need Mr. Bojangles. That's what she affectionately called the dildo that she got which had the same shape and length of Ren's dick. It was seven inches long, thick like a pickle, only difference was that it didn't radiate any heat like Ren's dick could.

Nina got out the tub and dried off thoroughly. She looked at herself in the full length mirror behind the door. The reflection of her mahogany brown skin radiated as she continued to stare at her body. Grabbing her breasts she noticed how they have gotten larger since she'd picked up the weight. She went from a 34b to a 36c. Feeling them closely like her doctor recommended, she made sure to check for any lumps. She looked at her body from all angles and loved what she saw. She had a brick-house-body that could rival any woman her age. Why couldn't Ren appreciate how fine she was, even with a little more weight? She could remember her mother and aunts saying that she needed to pick up more weight when she was younger. Now that she was thirty eight, she had hips, ass, and shapely legs to boot. She just had to find ways, like some new outfits, to get her man's attention.

She went into the closet and found a cute little sundress to put on. She grabbed some flip-flops to give her poor feet a break, plus she was going to Madame Chin's to get a pedicure and manicure. Grabbing a rubber band she fixed her braided hair into a ponytail and off she went.

***

Madame Chin's Nail Emporium was on Buckner Blvd. right before you get to Hwy 30. It was in a strip mall next to a Subway and an Allstate insurance office. When you walk in the shop, the first thing you smell is the strong scent of acrylic. Chin is usually at the front door to greet all of her customers. She is a tiny Philippine lady with eyebrows that look like they were penciled on in the dark. She always had that surprised look on her face like she just won the lottery.

"Hello Mrs. Love. What will it be today?" Chin asked smiling and bowing.

"I need the works sweetie," Nina replied with a slight chuckle.

"Okay. Your friend Mrs. Sanders is here. Would you like seat next to her?"

"Yeah. That'll be perfect."

Mrs. Chin led her to the back and Nina took a seat in a large leather recliner. She ran the hot water for her to soak her feet in, and she turned on the massage feature on the large leather chair. Keith's wife, and Nina's best friend Natalie, was already sitting there. She had her eyes closed while she was relaxing.

Natalie had that cute little girl next door look. She had a round face with these large dimples. She had big brown eyes that look like they could jump straight out of her head. She had full lips and a small pudgy nose. Her hair was cut short in a bob. Even though Natalie was a couple of years younger than Nina, she was very mature for her age.

"What's up big momma?" Nina said tapping the pregnant Natalie on the leg.

"Hey girl! You're here for the works too?"

"You know it. My dogs have been killing me. Plus I'm gettin hooked up for my big night with my man."

"Does he know it's a big night?" Natalie asked with a slight frown.

"He will when he comes home and sees me. I got it all planned out girlfriend. I'm going to make his favorite meal, have his bath water ready, put on some slow jams, cover the bed with rose petals, and I got me a brand new negligee from *Victoria Secret* that's sure to knock his socks off," she said, snapping her fingers from side to side.

"Girl you're doing a lot of extra shit when you don't have to. I dun told you what to do. You need to tighten up on your skills and give that man some good old fashion head. Betty Wright said it best," Natalie joked as she started singing. "Be a cook in the kitchen, a lady in the street, you can't show your teeth to every guy you meet, it's alright to be a little sweet but be a mother to the kids and you know what in the sheets. No pain, no pain, no gain."

Nina broke out in laughter, "You crazy girl!"

"I'm serious! You need to spice things up. I was watching Real Sex on HBO the other night. It was a chick on there teaching different techniques on how to give better head. She had this thing called the basket weaving technique. Where you grease your hands and rotate them around his dick while going up and down at the same time. Then she showed how to put a condom on with your mouth at the same time. I did that on Keith and he's been following behind my ass like a lost puppy dog ever since. I damn near have to push his' ass out the door 'cause he's all underneath me. I be like shit, move around, ain't the Cowboys playing or something!"

"I hear you, but I was raised different. My mom always said that nice girls never do that kinda thing."

"Child Please! That might've been true in the fifties when your momma was raised, but not now. Shit! You'd better start getting better acquainted with that dick of his." Natalie paused, "because I'll tell you what, there's plenty of women out here that will. You got some trifling ass hoes out there with no bounds that'll do any and everything thing they can to sink their claws into a good-man like Ren."

"Anyway, enough about me, how are you doing?"

"This baby is kicking like Bruce Lee. My back is hurting. I haven't seen my feet in a month. I got a strange craving for peanut butter, and I'm horny as hell."

"Yeah girl I remember those days. Have ya'll came up with a name for the baby yet?"

"Ah, I'm kind torn between Amarie and Zakiea."

"Both names are cute; you can't really go wrong with either one.

***

After they finished getting their nails done, Nina went home and started preparing Ren's favorite meal. She seasoned and broiled a nice juicy T-bone steak. She had already dropped Michael off at her mother's house, so they could have the whole place to themselves. In the bedroom, she tossed some rose petals on the bed. She ran some bath water and made it extra hot. That way by the time he got in, it would be just right. She put on her new laced bra and panty set with the matching robe and a pair of stilettos. Even though she couldn't stand him, Nina put on Ren's favorite singer, Prince. She went back to the bathroom one last time to straighten out her hair and sprayed on some of her Tresor perfume.

The door open and she heard Ren come in. She went to the kitchen to check on the steaks and the baked potatoes that she had placed in the oven earlier. Ren went into their bedroom and took a quick shower while she was setting up the dining room table. He never noticed the bed or the drawn bath water. He changed into some slacks and a button down shirt. Nina was in the dining room setting the table and putting a bottle of champagne in an ice bucket. Ren came back out and saw Nina as he was heading back to the front door.

"Hey baby what's goin on?" He asked planting a kiss on her cheek and checking out the ambiance of the dining room.

"Nothing much, just hooking up your favorite meal," she answered with a smile pointing to the candle lit table.

"Oh! Looks nice, but I'm sorry baby. I can't stay. I got some work to do."

"I thought we could spend some time together," she said in a pleading tone rubbing on his chest.

"So that's why you're playing some Prince, huh?"

"Yeah! I even got you a t-bone steak in the oven, medium rare just like you like it too."

"That sounds great, but I can't stay baby. I just had some stuff that came up at the last minute. Some work I gotta tend to. I'll make it up to you though, I promise. We'll go out to dinner this weekend. Keep the food warm for me. I'll try to get back as soon as I can."

"But ah…"

And before she could get out the words, Ren had half heartedly kissed her on the forehead and darted out the front door. She sat down at the table staring at the food. Cracking open the champagne, she took a swig right out the bottle. "So much for my big plans," she said slumping back into her chair.

CHAPTER 4

Heather wiped the sweat dripping from her forehead after her customary workout. Billy Blanks' Inspirational Taebo video had her feeling exhilarated after a sluggish morning. She had stayed up too late the night before watching all the episodes of *Lost* that she had recorded on her Tivo unit. Continuing to wipe down the rest of her body she glanced over at the clock on the living room wall and realized she was going to be late for her book club meeting. Quickly, she jumped in the shower and got dressed. Even in her hast to make her meeting on time, she made sure to clean the tub thoroughly and neatly put away the sweaty towel and leotard she was wearing. Being a stay at home housewife, her husband expected an immaculate home and that's just what she gives him. Picking out a sexy low cut dress, she slid back on her wedding ring, grabbed her car keys off the nightstand and headed for the garage. The brand new Lexus LS 450 that her husband brought her for Christmas had just been detailed and it sparkled from the rays of the sun as Heather opened the garage door and pulled out.

Slightly late, Heather arrived at Romano's to find that the other ladies had already been seated. The restaurant was still empty; the lunch rush hadn't started yet. It was quiet enough where Heather could hear the soft sound of mandolins playing in the background. Alerting the hostess that she was with the same party, the hostess grabbed an extra chair and placed it next to the table. "Bitches," she joked while straightening out her dress as she took a seat, "Sorry I'm late."

"That's okay girl. We're all running on C.P. time," Cynthia commented as she patted Heather on the arm. Cynthia was impeccably dressed as normal. The short skirt she was wearing with the slit on the side showed off her most prominent attribute, her incredibly long legs. Flipping her long beautiful hair back she reached into her purse and grabbed her small compact. Noticing her lipstick was uneven she used the napkin that was holding the silverware together to dab her sumptuous lips.

"What can I get you ladies to drink?" The waitress politely asked while she handed out menus.

"Just give me a Coke," Cynthia answered continuing to fix herself in the mirror.

"I'll take a glass of white wine," Heather answered tucking her purse away.

"Give me a Coke too," Monique replied.

"Okay I'll be right back with your drinks," the waitress announced as she briskly walked off.

"Where is Tina?" Cynthia inquired finally putting away the compact and looking up for the first time. "This is the second time she's missed a meeting."

"I don't know. She hasn't returned any of my calls or e-mails," Monique replied. Monique was a little more conservative than her book club mates. She's sporting her customary pant-suit and pumps. Even though she has a fabulous figure, she rarely shows it off. Always putting her career first, she feels it necessary to main-tain her professional image at all times.

"That's strange," Heather added.

"Certainly is, especially since she's the treasurer and the bitch has my money," Cynthia said rolling her eyes.

"Stop trippin Cindy! You never know what that girl might be going through. Remember the last time she was here, she had man problems. She could be dealing with that for all you know," Monique snapped.

"Man problems! Shit! I ain't letting no man stress me out like that," Cynthia commented sucking her teeth.

"Well, we all can't be like you, now can we?" Monique retorted folding her arms and tilting her head to the side.

"Don't hate me cause I got my choice of

sponsors. I say if the men play so can we," Cynthia remarked with a devilish grin.

"What about love?"

"What about it? Hey, all I need is a man with a big dick and big wallet."

"Wait a minute! Wait a minute," Heather interrupted, "what about that guy you met a month back, Andre? I thought you said you found out that he had no job and that he was living at home with his mother."

"Yeah that motherfucker is broke, but boy he's a pipe laying son-of-bitch. So I guess one out of two ain't bad. Hello!" Cynthia joked as she gave Heather a high five.

"You two need to stop it. You should be ashamed of yourselves. Try to show some decorum. We are in a restaurant for heaven's sake," Monique said turning her nose up at the ladies. Not a snob, but Monique considered herself to be sophisticated and she frowned when the ladies acted less than dignified, especially in public.

"Yeah, yeah, yeah, whatever! So, what about that other chick, Mrs. Goodie-two-shoes," Cynthia asked while making quotation marks with her fingers. "She hasn't come back."

"She won't be back. I think y'all rubbed her the wrong way when we discussed that last book a couple of months back," Heather stated as the waitress placed everyone's drinks in front of them. "I don't think she liked it."

"Toni Morrison! That was an excellent

book. If she had a problem with that, she doesn't belong in this book club anyway," Cynthia said angrily.

"As much as I hate to agree, I think Cindy might be right. Something about her is weird. I can't quite put my finger on it," Monique added.

"Like I said, I don't think she'll be back."

"Oh well," Cynthia said sucking her teeth.

"Look here, since Tina is not here, why don't we just reschedule for next week. That way we can all be here to select the next book we want to read. Agreed?" Heather stated as Cynthia and Monique nodded their heads in agreement. "Good, because I have an idea for the next book. It's called *Addicted* by Zane, and I've been dying to read it!"

***

After finishing her salad and breadsticks for lunch, Heather returned home and took a short nap before taking on the daunting task of cleaning the house. Although they had no children, the four bedroom, three-thousand square-foot home was a handful to keep clean. And being that Heather was a housewife, her husband expected perfection.

No sooner did Heather pull out her gloves and bucket did the phone rang. Walking into the kitchen, she grabbed the cordless phone. "Hello," she answered.

"Hey baby how's it going?" Her husband said on the other end.

"Just cleaning the house and getting ready for tonight. I can't wait to go to the *Studio Grill*. I heard this new Will Smith movie *I Am Legend* is suppose to be good. You're still coming home at six, right?"

"Well, that's what I'm calling about. You see I just picked up a big case. I mean big. And, eh, I'm going to have to work late," he replied.

"C'mon honey that's not fair. You promised we were going out tonight. You promised to spend some time with me."

"I know. But I just got this promotion baby. We talked about this remember? The sacrifices needed to further my career."

"Seems like I'm the only person doing the sacrificing."

"I'm sorry you feel that way, but I'm sacrificing too. I'm working day and night to provide a better life for you. That big house, that Lexus your driving, it takes money to buy those things baby. A little appreciation would be nice. Now I have to go. I'll see you when I get home," he said before hanging up abruptly.

Heather stood there with her arms folded biting her upper lip. She took off the gloves and began tapping her finely manicured nails against the granite kitchen countertop. "I'll show his ass," she said to herself. She picked up the phone and dialed.

"Hello."

"Ren," she said immediately perking up, "What's up baby?"

"Nothing much."

"What you got going on tonight?"

"Me and my boys are going to hang out at Johnny's."

"I need you tonight."

"Oh yeah!"

"Yes! Can I meet you up there? Please."

"Sure. What did you have in mind?"

"Role play. You see I've always had this fantasy that a stranger would pick me up in a bar, sweet talk me, and make wild passionate love to me."

"Shit! I can definitely be your stranger sweetie," Ren replied as his enthusiasm could be felt by Heather over the phone.

"So I can count on you to be there for me?"

"In the words of Michael Jackson, "I'll be there". You just wear that sexy red dress that I like."

"Anything for you baby."

CHAPTER 5

Johnny's Bar and Grill was predominantly a cop hang out. It was located on a sort of secluded lot in an industrial rundown neighborhood. The only business next to it, a meat packing plant, had closed down years ago. You would think that being secluded would make it a prime target to be hit by some knuckle heads, but Johnny's never had to worry about getting robbed. Those cops would fill some would be robbers with so much lead Superman couldn't see through them.

Johnny's was an older place that had lots of character. All the tables were made with solid oak. The bar was actually made of pure marble and it had brass handles to accentuate it. They didn't have a D.J, only a large juke box with everything from Marvin Gaye to Sting. On a Friday night, like tonight, it would be packed. Cops from every ethic back ground were welcomed, as long as they bleed blue. It's funny how the uniform can transcend race. It doesn't matter if you're a Jew, black, Mexican, or white. If you wear a shield you're accepted.

Half the guys were already there. Manny, Dwayne, and Jason had gotten themselves a table at the far corner of the bar. Sitting there waiting for Ren and Keith to show up, they ordered some beers and kicked back.

"So big boy, you gonna let your dick hang and talk to some women tonight or what?" Manny asked Dwayne.

"Man, I can't even think about that right now. I just got my first paycheck with the child support taken out of it. A hundred dollars a week, man, that shit hurts," Dwayne said like he was in pain.

"That's fucked up. She left you, got with another man, and on top of that you gotta kick her down with that kinda loot. You see that's why I'll never get married," Jason commented.

"You'll never get married 'cause nobody wants your ass," Manny joked. "And as far as the money goes, it's going to his kid."

"The hell it is! You watch Dwayne, all of sudden she'll be driving a brand new car, moving into a bigger house, and it'll be on your dime," Jason replied.

"Something's wrong with you. I mean something is really wrong with you to be telling Dwayne some dumb shit like that. You know Linda will make sure that every penny of that money is spent on junior," Manny rebutted.

"I don't know. Maybe Jason has a point. I mean that's an awful lot of money," Dwayne admitted.

"That's right! No way will she spend four hundred dollars a month on junior," Jason said shaking his head. "I'm telling you these mothers have gotten everyone, including the fathers and court system, fooled. Take it from me, I know. My sister has three kids. She gets child support from their two fathers totaling a thousand dollars a month. I've seen her take that money and spend it on everything from her car note, to getting a pedicure. Shit, I be hearing her laughing on the phone talking to her friends about how she can't wait to get her check 'cause she saw a new outfit at the mall she wanted!"

"There's always gonna be some women that abuse the system. But you got some women out there that are really struggling to make ends meet. That really need every dime to take care of their children," Manny noted.

"Oh yeah, like Will Smith's ex, who said she needs another ten thousand dollar increase 'cause she just can't quite make ends meet with the thirty thousand she's already getting a month," Jason said sarcastically. "Please! If the momma is struggling that damn much, give up the kid and let the daddy raise them. Remember both parents are supposed to be contributing equally, the key word being EQUALLY. If Dwayne here is kicking in four hundred dollars a month, do you honestly think that Linda is kicking in that same amount of money too?"

"Yeah! She's paying for rent, the electric bill, buying groceries and clothes, which is way more than just four hundred dollars a month I might add," Manny said.

"Last time I checked, junior don't eat no four hundred dollars a month in groceries, nor is he sporting a new outfit daily. And as far as those other bills go, she's going to pay rent and electric bills regardless," Jason added.

"Any way, this whole conversation is giving me tired head. We got off the main point, which is trying to get Dwayne some pussy tonight," Manny said ending the pointless debate that wasn't going anywhere.

"Yeah that's right. You never answered the question. Are you gonna let your dick hang tonight or what?" Jason asked.

"Maybe, I don't know," Dwayne replied leaning back in his chair and taking a deep breath.

"C'mon man. It's been over a year since Linda left you. She's moved on, now it's time you do the same. You need to start spending some time with other women instead of thinking about her ass," Manny said.

"I do talk to other women. Me and Janice from personnel kick it from time to time."

"Yeah! But are you fucking her?"

"Why are you all up in my business? I told you we kick it."

"Okay, that sounds cool and all, but do you wanna fuck her?" Manny and Jason were sitting at the edge of their seats with great anticipation like they were ten year old kids on the last day of school ready to breakout the classroom.

"I haven't thought about it."

"Bullshit!" They both yelled out slapping the palms of their hands on the table.

"You either want to fuck her or not," Jason explained.

"That's right! There's only two types of women in this world, the ones you fuck and the ones you don't. Which one is she?" Manny asked.

"Really man, I don't know if I'm ready," Dwayne said throwing up his arms.

Just then, Ren and Keith came strolling through the front door. "Gentlemen, what's up?" Ren said with exuberance.

"Nothing much boss, just trying to get down to the reason why Dwayne over here has put his dick in hibernation," Manny joked looking back and forth between Ren and Dwayne.

"You guys need to leave me the hell alone. I don't need ya'll help." Dwayne said appearing a bit agitated. He pulled out a can of Copenhagen, pinched off a piece, and shoved it in his gums. Grabbing an empty beer bottle he spit out the excess juice.

"Dwayne, my man, we gonna get you laid tonight," Ren declared putting his arm over Dwayne's shoulder. "The best way to get over an old flame is to start a new one."

"Hell yeah! Shit you guys know my motto,

ain't no pussy like new pussy," Manny inter-jected while pounding his fist against Jason's.

"Whatever," Dwayne responded shaking his head.

The waitress came over to take the guys or-ders. "What'll it be fellas?"

"Bring us a pitcher of beer, a bottle of bour-bon, and shot glasses for everyone. This round is on me boys," Ren said making a circle around the table with his finger. He pulled out his wal-let and sat down a crisp hundred-dollar bill on the table.

The guys all smiled and started whistling. She briskly walked off and got their drink order. Each of the guys poured themselves a drink and raised their shot glasses for a toast.

"Boys, this is for a job well done. Now it's time to reap the rewards for all our hard work. To the Ghost Squad."

"To the Ghost Squad," they all repeated.

Everybody smiled and banged glasses. All you saw was the bottom of the shot glasses as they all down their bourbon quickly, except for Keith. He half-heartedly raised his glass to the toast. He sat his drink down on the table with-out taking a sip. Most of the guys hadn't no-ticed except for Jason. Jason was checking out his mannerisms from the corner of his eye.

"You know while you're all in my fucking business; I got twenty bucks that says you can't pull a honey outta here that I pick for you," Dwayne said talking to Manny while slamming down the money on the table.

"You're on! Who you got in mind, big boy?" Manny asked.

"You see that little tender roni over there," Dwayne said pointing to a woman sitting at the bar. Her back was to them, so they couldn't see her face.

"No problem!" Manny replied pulling a twenty out of his pocket and slamming it on the table as well. He took one more drink of his beer, got up, and smoothly made his way over to the young woman.

"Watch this!" Dwayne said to Ren, elbowing him in the ribs and smiling.

Manny walked over with confidence. Straightening out his collar, he ran his fingers through his well oiled hair to make sure it was in place. He stopped for a second and checked her out more closely. She's a brunette with long hair. Her skin was beautifully tanned. She was wearing a burgundy dress with matching peep-toe pumps. Her legs were crossed and she was nursing a cosmopolitan. From behind she was as fine as any woman in there.

"Excuse me, but you're way too fine a woman to be sitting here alone. How about you and me get acquainted on the dance floor?" Manny asked reaching for her hand.

"I love to," she answered in a foreign accent, likely Russian, as she turned around.

"Goddamn!" Manny blurted in total shock. He made a face like he pulled up the zipper on his pants too fast. She looked horrible. Her face was covered with acne. She has a nose that is so fat that if she inhaled everyone else in the bar would suffocate to death. Her teeth were crooked like she chews on rocks for a snack, not to mention the fact that she is cross- eyed. Manny couldn't tell if she was looking at him or the man on the bar stool next to them.

"No, my name his Helen, but people keep mistaking me for this goddamn person. We must look a lot a like," she said stumbling through her words, like she just learned the English language last week.

The guys sitting at the table were on the floor laughing. None of them could keep their composure as they almost busted a gut. She grabbed Manny's hand and took him up on his offer. She led him to the dance floor. He held her close so that he could put his head on her shoulder. That way he doesn't have to look at her face.

Manny finally broke away after what seemed an eternity to him. It seemed like the juke box had the extended version of Whitney Houston's "I Will Always Love You," complete with piano and guitar solos. He got back to the table to find that the guys were laughing so hard, that they were in tears now.

"Here you go Manny. You win!" Dwayne joked pushing the money from the bet towards him.

"Ha, ha, motherfucker!" Manny said sarcastically. "I thought that damn song would never end!"

"It's about time you got a taste of your own medicine," Dwayne shot back.

"You need to stop hating man," Manny picked up his beer and took a swallow.

"Hating! Hating on what?"

Manny stood up and grabbed the lapel of the suit coat he was wearing. "Armani suit five-hundred dollars, Salvatore Ferragamo shoes four hundred sixteen dollars. Having a big dick and can get any woman I want, priceless. You better recognize," Manny said grabbing his manhood and smiling.

They all laughed themselves silly as Ren motioned for Dwayne and Manny to calm down.

"Okay guys. It's about time I show you all how it's done," Ren said. "Check out old girl over there."

Ren locked his eyes on this super fine look-ing lady at the bar who had just turned around. She was a strikingly good looking black woman. She had that light, bright, and damn near white looking skin, probably because she's mixed. From a distance, with her long black shoulder-length hair, she might be mistaken for a white woman, but the facial features never lie. Her high cheek bones, nose, and full lips told the story of her black heritage. A young woman, she was in her late twenties. She was tall and had an athletic build. Her chest was oozing out of her low cut dress like she was wearing a push-up bra. With a form-fitting blue *Donna Karan* strapless dress and spaghetti strapped stilettos to match, she was so hot when she crossed her legs you would've thought she could've started a fire.

"No way. No fucking way your ass is gonna pull primetime trim like that," Jason said shaking his head vigorously.

"Do I smell another bet?" Ren suggested with a sinister grin.

"Hell yes! I got twenty," Jason answered pulling out some money from his pockets. "Anybody else want some?"

Every guy, including Keith, put a twenty on the table. Ren took another sip of his bourbon as he stood up. The bourbon slid down his throat, spreading its wings causing him to lose his breath for a second. He pulled a can of Altoids out of his pocket, and popped three in his mouth. "Watch and observe," he ordered walking over to the young lady.

The young lady at the bar had placed an order with the bartender only moments before, and now he returned with her Sex on the Beach. He wiped down the counter, sat her drink on a coaster, and waited patiently as she grabbed her purse to pay him. Ren slowly walked up behind her. Surrounding her by putting his arms against the bar, he got real close as his cool breath slid down the back of her neck.

"I'll pay for that," Ren offered, handing the

bartender a folded ten dollar bill.

"You always buy strange women drinks?" she asked, without turning around.

"No! But for a woman like you, I'll definitely make an exception."

"Why am I so lucky?" She inquired further taking a sip of her drink.

"Because you're special."

"And how do you know that?"

"Call it male intuition. What's your name?"

"Heather. And you?"

"My name is Lorenzo, but my friends call me Ren."

"And what can I do for you officer Ren?" She sarcastically said as she finally turned around to face him smiling.

"Officer! What makes you think I'm a policeman?" Ren asked.

"Because every man that comes in here is a cop."

"Well you're right! And it just so happens that you're breaking the law right now."

"How do you figure? Because it's a crime to look this good. I've heard that line ten times already tonight," she said pulling the cherry by the stem from her drink and placing it inside her mouth seductively. She pulled out the stem seconds later to reveal that she had tied it in a knot inside her mouth, "Now that's a crime," she chuckled.

"Real cute! Now, you're guilty of in sighting a large uprising," Ren said with a devious looking smile.

"Really," she replied licking her lips sexily.

"Oh Yeah! It's a very serious offense. But I'll be willing to drop the charges if you." Then he leaned closer and whispered in her ear. She began to blush. Her face curled into a smile. She was turned on instantly. The inner part of her thighs was moist and her nipples hardened. Ren had done what he does so well, he verbally penetrated her.

"Stop it. You're so nasty Ren," she joked, softly tapping him on the shoulder. "I'm not that type of girl."

"Oh I think you are. You can't fool me baby. I read people for a living. I know you love nothing better than a nice big stiff one," Ren said as he moved closer where his cheek touched hers and he smoothly let his next words roll off his tongue, "And I got what you need."

"Ren, I want you right now. The hell with the role play," she said, rubbing the front of his pants tenderly.

"I won't make you wait baby. We can get out of here. I just wanna fuck with my boys over there first. I had to teach them a lesson on picking up women," Ren turned around and looked at the guys who were staring in amazement.

"Oh! And I'm your unknowing pawn, something for you to showcase?" She asked cutting her eyes at him.

"Be proud. I damn sure wouldn't showcase

someone who was ugly. C'mon let's get outta here baby." Ren grabbed her by the hand and led her by the table the guys were sitting at. They all had these dumbfounded looks on their faces as Ren casually strolled by and picked up the money in the center of the table. "Later boys!"

***

Ren and Heather got into their cars and rendezvoused at the nearby Howard Johnson Hotel. As soon as they hit the room the clothes came flying off. There was no small talk, no sitting around or fixing drinks. Within seconds of the door closing, Ren had her panties on the floor. Softly pushing her against the wall, he began to slowly and passionately kiss her neck. Heather's body was soft and silky, as the scent of aloe and papaya was pleasing to his nose. Working his way down her body stopping first at her breast, he let his tongue do circles around her pointed nipples. Then he slid his tongue down to her bellybutton. Her knees became so weak that she used the wall to lean on so she wouldn't lose her balance. Ren felt her becoming putty in his hands, so he dropped to his knees and easily picked her up and put her on his shoulders. Like I said, Ren was incredibly strong. He let his tongue probe inside the deepest regions of her sweet, tight pussy. Heather screamed out in pleasure as she wrapped her legs around him and her eyes rolled into the back of her head. Ren continued the magic he was making with his tongue as he sucked on her clit as if it was warm, melted chocolate.

She got off his shoulders and started to kiss on his broad chest while running her fingers down his washboard abs. She used her soft warm hands to gently rub on his rock hard dick. Sensually licking the mushroom shaped head of his dick, she gently massaged his balls simultaneously. Heather put a rubber in her mouth and rolled it on to his dick without the aid of her hands. She did everything that Nina was reluctant to do and Ren loved it.

Pulling her over to the bed, he got on top of her slowly. Sitting up for a second he admired her beautiful body for a moment. Smiling at him, she licked her lips in delight. Ren grabbed her legs and pushed them back. To be in control and dominate the sexual act is something that brings Ren much pleasure. He loves for his woman to be in the most submissive of positions, never on top for instance. Leaning over her, he gently guided himself into her petite body. She was tight so Ren took his time to make her feel relaxed as he continued to work his way in. The penetration of his dick put an arch in her back so deep that only her butt and shoulders still touched the mattress. She tried to run from him but he grabbed her legs and pulled her close so she could receive everything he had to offer. With her legs in the air, he grabbed her wrists and pinned them down so she couldn't move. Stroking slowly at first, his pace began to quicken and grew more vigorous as he got into a steady rhythm. Heather was already working on her second orgasm as her right leg started shaking uncontrollably. Flipping her over like she was a pancake that was cooked on one side, he got behind her doggystyle. He slapped her on the ass so hard you'd thought he left his handprint on her butt. She loved it. Heather liked nothing more than to be manhandled. She tried holding off that next orgasm as long as she could, but it was of no use. He was too deep, too hard, and too relentless to be denied. Pumping on her like he was drilling for oil, she could feel the head of him swelling inside her. She knew his orgasm was coming. She timed it just right so that they would both reach their climax together. Ren collapsed on his back trying to catch his breath after all of the hard work he just put in. Heather turned around to face Ren and propped her head up while she too was breathing heavily.

"Baby I'm tired of this once a week stuff. I miss you. When will we be able to be together all the time?" She asked sweetly lying next to Ren and rubbing his chest.

"Heather, ah, I like being around you. You're a good kid, but, ah, I'm a married man with a child that needs me. Plus I'm Catholic, and we don't believe in divorce," he said, sitting up and taking a drink of water. "Not to mention you're married too."

"I know, I know. I'm not asking for anything drastic like that, I just miss you baby. I miss being around you, feeling your touch, lying in your arms. I feel so lonely when you're not around. Since my husband got promoted to his new job, it leaves me alone all the time."

"Hey, hey, hey, you know the rules. No talking about spouses when we're together."

"I'm sorry. I just wanna spend more time with you baby."

"I'll try to make more time to spend with you. I promise," Ren said kissing her on the forehead. "But you really need to find a hobby or something. I don't know...maybe knitting or join a book club or something."

"Actually, I did join a book club a few months back, *The Ladies of Distinction*. We're about to start on our fourth book."

"That's good!"

"Yeah, but a good book is no replacement for a good man."

CHAPTER 6

Monique was beginning to feel very tipsy. She was working on her fourth drink. The bartender had just brought over another gin and juice per her request. She and her co-workers were celebrating a night out on the town. They had just closed the biggest account in Braddock and Thompson history. Martin Electronics decided to let her agency handle their multi-million dollar ad campaign. Running point on the whole deal, Monique spent countless nights putting together an excellent presentation. Martin's board of directors was so impressed they actually stood and applauded when she finished. So with that bit of good news, she decided to let her hair down for once and enjoy a night out with the gang.

Monique was a lovely woman. She was thirty, with honey brown skin, light brown eyes, and long hair that came down to her shoulders. She was a very voluptuous woman who had a lot of curves that gave her a great figure. Her double-d chest had men constantly staring at her, especially tonight where she was being hit on relentlessly. But she really didn't want any part of a man right now since she had just broken up with someone three months back. She hadn't gotten over him yet.

Sitting next to Monique at the bar was Vickie. Vickie was not only Monique's co-worker but also her best friend. While Monique was irritated at the mere sight of a man, Vickie was on the prowl. She was extremely flirtatious this evening. She had been making eye contact with a fellow at the other end of the bar. He called over the bartender and asked him to send Vickie a drink. After Vickie took a few sips of her Hypnotic, she continued to flirt with the man. She ran her index finger around the rim of the glass she was drinking and licked her finger sexily while staring at him.

"What are you doing Vickie?" Monique asked as she leaned over and talked loudly in her ear because of the loud music that was playing in the background.

"Getting my mack on. Shit. Look at him, he's fine," Vickie replied grinning ear to ear.

"So what happened to, we don't need men tonight? That tonight it's about us girls?"

"Did you hear me when I said that he's fine?"

"I told you I just wanted to celebrate the new account with a couple of drinks; I'm not interested in meeting any men."

"C'mon Monique, just because you had problems with your mystery man, is no reason to kill my buzz. It's been four months since I had me some, and I need to release some pressure damn-it," Vickie said snapping her fingers. "What does it matter to you anyway?"

"Because he's over there with his ugly friend, and men are like dogs, they travel in packs," Monique pointed out sucking her teeth.

Sure enough, the guy Vickie was flirting with stood up and began making his way over through the crowd with his friend following closely behind. The guy that Vickie was flirting with walked over with a big smile as he started talking to her. While the other man straighten up his shirt and fiddled with his watch as he summed up the courage to come talk to Monique.

"Excuse me baby, but you look familiar. Haven't we met somewhere before?" He asked flashing a smile showing all of his pearly-whites.

"Yes we have. That's why I don't go there any more," she snapped rolling her eyes.

"C'mon baby, don't be like that. My name is Alexander," he said in a strange accent.

"Alexander, hmm…what kind of accent is that Alex?"

"Pardon me, I'm sorry. I've been living in France for the past three years. I got use to speaking French all the time. I must have picked up the accent," he replied.

"So you speak French huh?"

"Oui," he answered in French with a

smooth grin.

"Oh, okay. I speak it too...I studied it when I was at Princeton. Comment allez-vous?" Monique asked in her fluid French dialect.

"Ahhh...." The brother said dumbfounded, having no idea what she just said.

"Just like I thought, you haven't been anywhere close to France negro. Beat it."

The guy, who wasn't that bad looking, walked away completely defeated after being exposed for a fraud. Monique didn't even bother covering her mouth while snickering at him. Drinking the last of her gin and juice, she turned and looked at Vickie who was still hamming it up with oh boy. Walking over Monique whispered in her ear, "Vickie I'm ready to go."

"Give me a minute sweetie," Vickie said to the man who was hovering over her.

"C'mon Monique, hang out a little while longer. We're just getting acquainted."

"Nah, it's been a long day. I'm ready to go home. You can stay if you want; but I'm calling a cab."

"Are you sure?" Vickie asked.

"Yeah, you have fun. I'm going to turn in," Monique answered as she started yawning.

"Thanks, I really appreciate it. I'm going to make it up to you. Next weekend we'll go to the spa at the Four Seasons, on me."

"I'm going to hold you to that," Monique said smiling as she grabbed the bartender and asked him to call her a cab.

The cab met her in front of the bar about twenty minutes later and dropped her off at the corner of her apartment building. She gave him a five dollar tip and headed for the security gate where you needed a card to enter the complex. It was quiet, not another soul in sight. It was also dark; the only light was coming from a small street lamp that was on the sidewalk a couple of feet away. Monique by now was as high as a kit. She almost floated over to the gate. She opened her purse to look for her key-card so she could scan it to open the gate. Stepping out of the shadows from the side of the building was a mysterious stranger. She was still fumbling through her purse and didn't hear the person creeping up behind her.

"Need some help?" The stranger asked.

She turned to see who was asking her this question. She couldn't make out anything about the person, as she strained her eyes in the dark. Who ever it was lurking in the shadows was dressed in all black and wrapped in the cloak of the night. The only thing visible was the silhouette that the small street lamp provided.

"No I'm okay," Monique eventually replied.

Monique was getting nervous. In her drunken state she hadn't realized just how desolate the area was around her apartment. Glancing at the eerily quiet street, she realized that no one else was around. Not even a random car coming down the boulevard to break the silence. She frantically shifted through her purse with much more urgency now. Her fingers finally ran across the key card. She pulled it out quickly and turned back to the gate. The mysterious figure moved toward her when she turned her back and a long sharp knife came out of nowhere. The stranger reached back with the blade and before Monique even knew what happened, she was slashed in the back of her neck with great force. Blood came squirting out everywhere. Monique fell to her knees holding the back of her neck as the blood poured through her hands. In extreme pain on all fours, she tried her best to escape the stranger by crawling away and yelling for help. But her cries went unheard as the mysterious person stepped out of the darkness and into the light where Monique could see the face of her attacker more clearly.

"It's you!" Monique said between gasp for air, as her eyes opened so wide you would have thought they were going to pop out of her head.

Before she could get out another word, the figure bent down, grabbed Monique by the top of her hair, and slashed her again in the front of her throat. She fell backwards gasping for air and holding her throat. Her small hands couldn't stop the large gash in her neck from squirting out blood. She yelled for help again, but the blood had quickly begun to fill up her lungs. Taking one last gasp, she fell lifelessly to the concrete.

CHAPTER 7

The phone rang at the house of Franklin McCain about four in the morning. He was no stranger to getting calls that early being a homicide detective. Fumbling around his nightstand in the dark he searched for the receiver. After knocking everything over, including the lamp, he finally found it and answered the phone.

"Hello," he said still half asleep.

"McCain this is Evans the Watch Commander. I'm sorry to disturb you, but your next in rotation."

"I thought it was Jones turn," he said still trying to collect himself.

"He was. It's been a busy night. There was another murder earlier tonight that he caught. This one is yours buddy. You got a pen and paper so I can give you this address?"

"Ah, I got a photographic memory, just spit it out."

"Okay, it's 5467 Buckner Blvd. You got it?"
"Got it!"

Hanging up the phone he slowly rolled out of bed. His joints cracked like the old wood that's on the floor boards of his townhouse. Making his way over to his old-fashion record player, he flipped through his albums and found some Frank Sinatra. Carefully placing the needle on the record so that he wouldn't scratch it, McCain puts on his favorite song that he listens to every morning while getting dressed, *Fly Me to the Moon*. He walked over to his large fishtank and took off the lid. "Hello babies," he said talking to the fish as sprinkled a little food into the water. He tapped on the glass and gazed at his goldfish as they started to feast on the food.

Flipping on the bathroom lights he glanced at himself in the mirror and saw that his brown eyes were bloodshot red. Putting some drops of Visine in his eyes, he grabbed some mini scissors from the medicine cabinet and commenced to trimming his mustache that had began to grow over his lips. After cleaning up, he strolled over to the closet and pulled out a suit that was older than most of the young policemen that he worked with. In no time flat, he was out the door and on his way to the crime scene.

McCain was a thirty year veteran of the Dallas Police Department with less than a year to go from mandatory retirement. He is a dedicated detective that has sacrificed everything for the job, including three marriages that failed miserably. A cranky old Irishman, McCain preferred to work alone, and because of his clout, he's the only detective at The Ship that can get away without having a partner.

McCain arrived at the scene to find it packed with people. The residents of the apartment complex were outside in their nightwear being nosey. News reporters searching for the next story already had cameras rolling as they tried to find out any little detail they could. Uniformed cops had sealed off the area with caution tape and didn't allow any of them thru, even other cops unless they had proper identification. It was still dark out, so they position fluorescent spot-lights around the crime scene so the detectives could see better. McCain flashed his badge and crossed the yellow tape. He walked over to the Sergeant who was in charge.

"What do we got?" McCain asked running his fingers through his thin gray hair.

"We got a DOA that was reported about an hour ago. Her throat was slashed and her hands were severed and removed. We haven't been able to locate them so far. There were no witnesses. The victim has no identification and since her hands were cut off, looks like we'll have to use dental records to identify the body. Joan from the medical examiner's office is already here," he read off a note pad while leading McCain to the victim.

"Okay. I want a team to do a canvas of the neighborhood, let's make it about a two mile radius. And let's get a second team searching for those hands. If they're out here I want them found."

"Yes sir."

McCain reached into his coat pocket and pulled out a pair of latex gloves. He slowly walked over to the victim and squatted down next to her. Joan was already taking her body temperature.

"McCain! I would've thought you were retired and on a beach somewhere living it up by now."

"I would have if I didn't have to finance my ex's retirement first," he said showing a rare grin. "So Joan what's the time of death?"

"Judging by the body temperature and the fact that rigor mortis hasn't set in yet, about two o'clock."

He moved closer and examined her arms. "What about the hands?"

"I can't give you a definite yet until I get her back to my table, but it looks like they were cut off postmortem."

"Any sign of rape?"

"There is no bruising or torn clothing to suggest it. But to error on the side of caution, I'll order a rape kit just in case."

McCain nodded his head as he observed closely and saw a piece of paper sticking from out of the shoe of the victim. Carefully, he slid off her high-heel shoe and pulled out a small piece of paper that was neatly folded. He opened it to see the message that had been typed on it.

"The hands that touch me will never touch another."

McCain studied the paper for a minute with a puzzled expression. In the corner of the paper was the number 140. "Interesting," McCain said as he pulled out a plastic evidence bag and put it inside.

"Sergeant!"

"Yes sir."

"Get this over to the lab. I want the prints ran on this. And make sure it's marked priority."

"Yes sir."

"So what are you thinking McCain? I know that wheel in your head is already spinning," Joan inquired, watched the boys wrap up the body and place it on the stretcher.

"Well, I have a young lady killed in front of her home, and her body left in plain view. I have a crime-scene with absolutely no signs of a struggle. I think the victim knew her attacker. And it had to be someone she was really close to because the way she was killed seems very personal."

"What makes you think it was personal?"

"Have you ever killed someone Joan?"

"No, I only like to examine them."

"Well I've had the unfortunate duty of using my service-revolver to shoot six assailants during my thirty years on the force. Four of them died. But none of those deaths bother me as much as when I killed a man in Vietnam. It was 1968 Saigon, my first *tour of duty.* We were ambushed one night. They had me and my squad pinned down in our foxholes. We held them off as long as we could, but we started to run out of ammunition. We began fighting hand to hand. This one gook rushed me and I stuck him with my bayonet. I must have hit him just right, you know between the bones of the rib-cage, because the blade easily slid into his chest. He stared at me and said something, but I didn't understand Vietnamese. His blood covered my hands as the shock of killing a man for the first time shook me to my soul. I said that to say this. Shooting a man, throwing someone out a window, poisoning their food is so impersonal. But walking up to somebody you know, sticking a blade in them, getting their blood on your hands, and looking them directly in the eyes when you do it. Well, nothing gets more personal than that."

***

Ren arrived at The Ship the next morning in a good mood. He'd gotten some good loving from Heather the night before, and caught no flack from Nina when he got back home. He had a quarter of a million dollars stashed away in a safety deposit box. His promotion was only a formality now. Yes it's easy to say that Ren was on cloud nine.

Then, he walked into The Ship.

"Ren can I see you in my office for a minute?" The Captain asked as he approached Ren.

"Yes sir."

He walked in and there was another guy already in his office. A tall white man with jet black hair, very slim, and well dressed in what looked like a tailor made suit.

"What's going on Captain?" Ren questioned sizing up the strange man with his arms folded.

"This is Lieutenant Greg Stanton of Internal Affairs. He's doing an investigation into the Morris Jones Shooting."

Stanton had been in Internal Affairs for less than a year. On the fast track to making Captain because of his connections, Stanton was from a prominent family, which is to say he's rich. His father was a cop until he finished law school. Now he is a senior partner for a prestigious law firm. His grandfather used to be an Assistant Police Chief before resigning and winning a seat in the state senate. Stanton is continuing the family tradition of becoming a cop. Partly because that was the stipulation that his parents put on him before he could get his inheritance. And it would look good on his resume when he leaves and follows his true ambition of one day running for Mayor.

"Pleasure to meet you Detective Love; I've heard a lot of good things about you," Stanton said shaking Ren's hand firmly. "I'm not here to step on anybody's toes. The Jones' lawyer has some pull in the city council. They've pressured the Chief into ordering an investigation to make sure that everything was by the book."

"I understand. What do you need from me?" Ren asked with a forced smile. Despite his hatred for Internal Affairs, he never let his true emotions show.

"Well, I need to interview your entire squad as soon as possible."

"No problem. I'll make sure all of my guys are available."

"I appreciate that."

"Stanton we're about to have roll call. As soon as we're finished you can use my office to conduct your interviews," the Captain added looking at his watch.

"Sounds like a plan," Stanton responded with a smile.

Ren left the Captain's office and immediately went to the club house. Everybody except Keith was already there. The guys were sitting around with their feet up checking out the morning news.

"Well, well, well! Here he is, the ladies man," Jason joked walking up and putting his arm around Ren's shoulder.

"So what happened?" Manny inquired playfully punching Ren in his other arm.

"You guys know me. I'm not the type to kiss and tell," Ren replied with a wink.

"C'mon Ren, I know you're not going to leave us hanging like that?" Jason inquired.

"Let's just say that she had a nice big stiff one. And I ain't talking about the drinks," Ren joked.

"Ain't you worried about her getting too close?" Manny added.

"Nope! Not with this chick. She's married too. You see that's the key. To be with someone that has just as much to lose as you. Then they'll be more likely to keep their mouth shut," Ren replied with a grin.

"Scared of Nina huh? You know she ain't having that shit," Jason joked.

"Obviously you boys don't recognize who wears the pants in my family. If I let Nina sit her pretty little ass on my face after she ate a whole plate of refried beans, she would not let out a fart without my permission."

The guys cracked up laughing. Ren walked over to the door and locked it. "All jokes aside, we got serious business to get down to ladies. Has anybody heard or seen Keith this morning?"

The guys all shook their heads no.

"Okay, I'll fill him in later," he said, pausing as his face got serious. "We got some serious business. Internal Affairs is here investigating the Momo shooting. We knew this was coming. Everybody needs to just stick with the story. Got it!" Ren urged keeping his voice low.

They all nodded their heads in agreement. A knock at the door startled them as Ren took his time unlocking it.

"Captain told me to tell you it's time for roll call," a uniform cop informed them sticking his head through the door.

"Thanks," Ren said as he closed the door and quickly turned back to the guys. "He's going to interview each one of us once roll call breaks. So be ready."

He reopened the door and the guys followed him into the meeting room. The other officers had taken their seats. Ren and the boys were the last ones in. Stanton was standing in the far corner studying the demeanor of the fellows as they walked in. The Captain took the podium with Detective McCain by his side.

"Ladies and gentlemen last night we had a brutal murder of a Jane Doe. Her throat was slashed and her hands were cut off. She was found in front of Brentwood Apt. on Buckner Blvd. We need everyone's ears to the street on this one. Her photograph is in the packet in front of you along with a physical description. McCain is running point on this investigation. All information is to be funneled through him. Any questions?"

Everybody remained silent.

"No! Then you're dismissed," the Captain said quickly leaving the podium.

Stanton shifted his way through the people and walked up to Ren, "If you're ready, I'll interview you first."

"Sure, give me minute," Ren said never looking up as he continued to study the photograph of the victim closely.

Ren walked over to McCain's desk. McCain had on his reading glasses and was hard at work. He was looking at the M.E's report that was just sent to him by Joan who had work on the autopsy overnight. She expedited it because of the importance.

"What's going on McCain?"

He looked up and saw that it was Ren and kept working.

"What was the cause of death on your Jane Doe?"

"What's it to you?" McCain replied sarcastically.

"Just want to do my part to help in the investigation."

"Look here Ren, I don't need your type of help."

"What the hell is that supposed to mean?" Ren asked as he bent down and put his hands on McCain's desk, trying to make eye contact.

"You know exactly what it means," McCain said never looking up. He continued to read the report as if Ren wasn't even standing there. "I don't need your kind of questionable tactics involved in my case."

"Look, my tactics might be physical and more confrontational than yours, but I get results none the less. Now all I wanna do is assist you. I know you're running the show."

McCain took off his reading glasses and looked Ren in the eyes for the first time. "As long as you realize that. She choked to death on her own blood. The hands were cut off post mortem. We have no witnesses. We're running her dental records now. We hope to have an ID on the vic by the end of business. Good enough?"

"Hey I'm just trying to help. Remember we're on the same side," Ren reiterated with his hands up in the air walking backwards heading towards the Captain's office. When he stepped in the office, he saw Stanton taking a seat behind the Captain's desk as he pulled out a tape recorder, notebook and pen ready to take notes.

"Okay Ren, I'm going to tape this interview. So why don't we start at the beginning. Tell me exactly what happen when you arrived at the house?" That was the question Stanton asked each of the men one after another. Ren, Jason, Dwayne, and Manny all ran down the same story as if they were reading from a script.

We arrived at Mr. Jones' house at eight in the morning to execute a warrant for his arrest for possession with and intent to deliver. We suited up with vest clearly marked police. Manny and Keith took the rear; Jason and Ren were on the front door. Dwayne was back up. We kicked in the door and yelled police. Momo was sitting on the couch and reached for his weapon. He fired a single shot at the door, and Ren returned fire hitting him twice in the chest.

Each man told the same story verbatim. They said it so often and with such great precision that you would have thought it really happened that way. They left no room for doubt. The story seemed iron clad. Yet Stanton was sitting there listing to the testimony scratching his head with a look on his face like he was trying to find the next piece to a puzzle. It was only one person left to interview, and that's Keith. He still hadn't shown up to work.

***

After the interviews, the squad met up at a nearby park. So they could be clear of the watchful eye of Stanton. Plus, Ren never liked to talk squad business in The Ship unless absolutely necessary.

"So how did it go?" Ren asked everyone.

"It went fine, just like we rehearsed," Dwayne said.

"Yeah, I mean he really didn't ask me too many questions," Jason added.

"You guys sure he didn't ask any strange questions?" Ren asked rubbing the back of his neck.

"No. He basically just took notes while I was in there," Manny said with Jason and Dwayne nodding their heads in agreement.

"Anybody got anything on Momo's successor yet?"

"Word on the street is that his younger brother, Red, has taken over." Dwayne said.

"You know where he rests his head at?"

"He's got no known address, but he owns a barbershop on Elam called Tight Cuts."

"Okay let's pay the *heir-apparent* a little visit."

Then Ren's phone began to ring. He looked at the caller ID and saw it was Keith. "Where are you at? You missed roll call."

"Natalie had a scare. We thought she was going into labor. It was false alarm though," Keith answered.

"I need to talk to you ASAP. Meet me at location blue in thirty minutes."

"I'll be there."

Ren hung up the phone. "I'm gonna hook up with Keith right quick. I'll meet you guys at the barber shop in an hour."

***

When Ren pulled into the Eleventh St. Park, Keith was already there sitting on the bench. He was calmly drinking a cup of coffee. Except for an older gentleman walking his little pooch, the park was pretty much empty. Ren hopped out of his car and briskly walked over. He knew he didn't have much time. Stanton was already suspicious that Keith wasn't there for the interviews with the rest of them. Ren knew that the more time passed, the more his suspicions would grow.

"Keith, I don't have much time because you gotta get back to The Ship in a hurry. So listen closely. A guy named Greg Stanton from Internal Affairs is at The Ship waiting to interview you about the Momo shooting. You need to go in there and tell the story just how we rehearsed it."

"Ren, man, I don't...." Keith murmured looking at his shoes before Ren interrupted him.

"Look I know how you feel. This is the last time you'll ever have to talk about it. Once all our stories match up, there'll be nothing more to investigate and the case will be closed for good. The rest of us have been interviewed already. You're the last one. He's waiting for you now. Just go to the Ship and get it over with," Ren said in a gentle voice as not to upset Keith.

Keith let out a deep sigh while rubbing his face. "Okay!"

CHAPTER 8

McCain had been sitting at his desk studying the Medical Examiner's report all afternoon with it in one hand and a cup of coffee in the other. He's been hard at work since he first hit the crime scene at a quarter after four this morning. Flipping back and forth from the report to the photos of the crime scene he continued looking for anything he had missed. Then McCain had noticed something. He held the photograph close to his face and looked at her shoes. It was amazing that he hadn't noticed it yet. Her shoes were on the wrong feet. McCain went to the Captain's office to fill him in on the developments. He knocked on the cracked door and let himself in.

"McCain! I'm glad you're here. I got some news for you. The ID came back on your Jane Doe. Forensics was able to use her dental records to identify her," the Captain said handing McCain the information. "Her name is Monique Harris. She lives in the building where she was found dead in front of. I've already had her phone records pulled. We should have them within the hour. I've sent CSU to her place to run prints. You need to get over there and try to find out her next of kin so we can notify them. And more important, find out where she was coming from the night of the murder," the Captain said taking a seat behind his desk.

"I'm on it, but check this out," McCain showed him the crime scene photo. "Her shoes were on the wrong feet, the killer must have switched them."

"You got any idea what this means?" The Captain asked inspecting the photos.

"I don't know yet, but this further supports my suspicions that the killer knew the victim and is intentionally leaving us clues."

McCain arrived at Monique Harris' apartment building to find that the uniform cops had already sealed off the immediate area surrounding her place. The yellow tape was up as nosey tenants stood outside their apartment doors trying to catch a glimpse. He made his way upstairs to her second floor apartment to see the Crime Scene Unit was already there dusting for finger prints. As soon as he opened the door, a cat jumped out of nowhere and startled him.

"Sorry about that detective. We called animal control to pick up the cat. He's been sitting in his little bed, so we left him alone," one of the investigators said lifting the finger prints off one of the door knobs to a random closet.

"Just keep him away from me. I hate cats,"

he said giving the cat a dirty look.

The cat darted into the bedroom as McCain refocused his attention on the task at hand. Walking through her living room he surveyed her home and carefully examined every little object. Monique's place was clean but cluttered. She was a pack rat. She had lots of furniture and keepsakes. That along with the fact that her living room was full of books made her place feel tiny. McCain walked over to her desk and began to look through her things. He found her phonebook and started thumbing through the pages. The numbers for her relatives and job were in there, but no sign of any love interest. Picking up the phone on her desk he called the Captain and gave him Monique's contact information so he could inform the family of the death.

After hanging up the phone, he searched the rest of the apartment a while longer and came up with nothing. He decided to head down to the offices of Braddock and Thompson and conduct interviews with her boss and co-workers. Their offices were located on the sixth floor of the prestigious Myerson building downtown. Entering the huge lobby with a view of the downtown skyline, he walked over to the secretary's desk and flashed his badge.

"Excuse me Ma'am. I need to speak to the person in charge," he said in that calm demeanor of his.

"Yes sir. Just a minute please," she picked

up the phone and called someone to the front. A short pale face white man with a receding hairline walked up with a courteous smile that looked like it was forced.

"Hello my name Dennis Bay, how can I help you sir?" He said politely shaking McCain's hand.

"You have some place where we can talk privately?" McCain asked.

"Sure! Follow me," he turned and led McCain to a vacant meeting room.

McCain hated this part of the job. He always cringed at the idea of delivering bad news to friends and loved ones. It's probably how he got all those lines and wrinkles in his face.

"Does a Monique Harris work here?"

"Yes. Matter of fact, we've been concerned about her. She hasn't shown up for work yet. It's not like her to not show up or call."

"I'm sorry to tell you this, but she was murdered last night."

Dennis stood there with his mouth wide open in total shock. His pale face became flush in seconds. "I don't believe it! We just went out last night to celebrate getting this big account."

"Was Ms. Harris there?" McCain asked staying focused despite Dennis' grief.

"Yes we went to Ray's Room on lower Greenville Ave. We had a few drinks. She got a ride there with her friend and co-worker Vickie," Dennis answered doing his best to keep his composure.

"Is Vickie here now?"

"Yes sir. I'll go get her for you."

"While you're getting her, can I see Ms. Harris' office?"

He nodded his head and led McCain to Monique's office. McCain sat behind her desk and started going through her e-mails, but he found nothing but generic messages. There was an e-mail from her mother reminding her that her brother's birthday is next week. There was one from her sister Janet, which had the best comebacks to terrible pickup lines. Nothing had a threatening tone to it though. He scanned through all of her personal office correspondence, but nothing looked suspicious there either. A few minutes later Vickie walked in crying her heart out. McCain hopped up and went over to briefly console her. He put his arm on her shoulder, and led her to the leather couch that was against the wall. Pulling out a handkerchief from his pocket he politely offered it to her.

"I'm sorry for your lost. I know this is a difficult time for you. We're going to do everything we can to find her killer. But first, I need your help; I gotta ask you a few questions, while the information is fresh in your head."

She nodded her head while blowing her nose. McCain stood up and pulled his notepad out of his pocket. "Mr. Bay said that Monique caught a ride with you to the bar?"

"Yes. She rode with me. And if I would

have left when she wanted to instead of letting her catch a cab, she'd still be alive right now," Vickie said, breaking down and crying even harder.

"You two were pretty close huh?"

"We were best friends."

"Did anyone bother her at the bar?"

"Guys were hitting on both of us. You know, normal bar stuff."

"Did she have any enemies you can think of?"

"No! Monique is the sweetest person you would ever meet. I can't imagine anyone having a problem with her."

"What about a boyfriend? Has she been seeing anyone in particular?"

"She was seeing someone that she just broke up with. I think he was married, because she would never bring him around or let me meet him. Everything that she did with him was a damn secret. She never even told me his name. She referred to him as only L."

"Thank you. You've been a big help. If you can think of anything else give me call," he said pulling out a business card and handed it to her.

***

Keith came strolling in the front door of The Ship, he casually made his way into the Captain's office. The Captain was gone, but Stanton was sitting behind his desk looking over some notes. His suit jacket was hanging on the back of the chair and his sleeves were rolled up. He was feverishly at work when Keith walked in.

"Excuse me. Is Captain Riley anywhere around?"

"Let me guess. You're Detective Sanders?"

"Yes."

Stanton got up and walked over to shake his hand. "I've been expecting you. I'm Greg Stanton with Internal Affairs. Please, have a seat detective."

Keith had that customary look of indifference on his face that he wears like a pair of sunglasses. He slowly takes a seat as he looks around curiously. "I'm sorry that I'm late. My wife is pregnant and we had to see the doctor this morning."

"No problem. As you can see I had a little paperwork to go over anyway," Stanton said walking back behind the desk and taking a seat. "Like I told the other members of your squad, I'm here on behalf of the chief to make sure that the Jones case was handled by the book. I just wanna make sure there's no loose strings that can be pulled on. The chief doesn't want to give the Jones family any reason to question police tactics."

"Sure. I understand," Keith said nervously rubbing his mustache.

"I have to tape this interview," Stanton said pulling out his mini recorder and putting in a new tape. "Okay let's start from the beginning. Tell me what happened when you first arrived at the scene if you don't mind."

Just like the previous guys from the Ghost Squad, Keith began telling the story. And just like the others, every detail was the same. He had done like Ren requested. But there was something different now. Keith's mannerisms were strange. He was constantly moving around in his chair like an eight year old with ADD. On top of that, he never looked at Stanton while he told his story. This made Stanton suspicious. Stanton was a master at facial recognition. He taught the class for new recruits before he was promoted to Internal Affairs. He could sniff out a liar much like a blood hound could pickup a scent.

"So that I get this right, you and Manny secured the rear entrance. Mr. Jones was in the living room and he pulled his weapon out on Ren and Jason as they hit the front door. He opened fired on Ren and he returned fire hitting him twice in the chest."

"Yes sir."

"Once he was hit with the two shots, who secured Mr. Jones' weapon?"

"I believe Jason did."

"Okay that's all I need from you. If you think of anything else give me call," Stanton informed Keith as he offered him a business card.

Stanton was now convinced that the Ghost squad was hiding something. He didn't know what it was, but he wasn't ending this investigation until he found out what.

***

Ren met back up with the boys at Tight Cuts. The barbershop was in a rundown looking strip mall. It was in the corner suite next to a daycare center. The parking lot was full of potholes, and the paint on the building was peeling. Despite the appearance, the barbershop thrived.

Standing outside on either side of the front door was two of Red's guards. Both men, who are large in stature, were chatting as they noticed the Ghost Squad approaching. Ren walked up first with the rest of the guys following closely behind. One of the guys guarding the door stepped in front to prevent them from just walking in.

"What the fuck you want?" The guard barked in a loud intimidating tone.

"We need to talk to Red, so stand aside."

"I don't think so. No po po allowed," he said putting his hand on Ren's chest to prevent him from walking forward.

"I think you need to get your ears cleaned, because you didn't hear me."

Then with an extreme swiftness so fast that if you blinked your eyes you would've missed it. He grabbed the hand that was placed on his chest and twisted it to bring him to submissive position. Then with his open right hand, he hits the guard in the Adam's apple and he falls to the floor gasping for breath and holding his wrist in pain.

"You should get that looked at," Ren suggested sarcastically as he casually stepped over his body. Dwayne walked up to the other guard who was standing there in amazement at what just happened to his partner. Dwayne, who was stone face, grabbed the man's shirt collar with those big meat hooks he calls hands and asked in that infamous voice of his, "We're not gonna have a problem with you, are we?"

The guard once again glanced over at his partner who was still on the ground in pain and then his eyes came back over and focused in on the massive arms of Dwayne's that looked like they were going to rip through his shirt like Bruce Banner turning into the *Incredible Hulk*. He just shook his head no and Dwayne tossed him aside like wet rag.

The shop was pretty much vacant this time of day. A couple of the barbers were playing dominoes and listening to the local radio station. Sitting in the far barber chair getting a razor shave was Jamal 'Red' Jones. Red was the younger brother of Momo. He's the opposite of Momo. Where Momo was refined, even tempered, and an astute businessman, Red was thuggish, highly volatile, and made decisions off pure emotion. They even looked different. Red was much taller, he's stocky, and he has nappy red hair hence the nickname Red. Not only did they look and act different, they also dressed different. Momo loved nothing better than the look of tailor made Italian silk suit with gold cuff links and a pair of Stacy Adams shoes. Red, on the other hand, liked wearing extra long t-shirts, wave caps, and blue jean shorts that sag so low, that every time Red took two steps he would have to pull them back up to keep them from falling around his ankles. He's relaxing in his chair with his eyes closed as the barber finishes his shave when Ren and the Ghost Squad walked up.

"Hey Red! How's it going? You know your guys outside have no manners. We had to let ourselves in."

Red sat up in his chair and opened his eyes. "What the fuck y'all doing in my place?" Red asked as he stood up and threw off the towel that was tucked under his chin.

"Word on the street is you're the new king."

"You gotta lotta fucking nerve bring your black ass in here after killing my brother, chump!"

"Your brother should have never drawn down on a cop."

"Bullshit! I know my brother. He ain't stupid. He would've never drawn down on a cop!"

"Listen up," Ren stepped closer to Red and lowered his voice so that only he could hear him. "I'm not here to talk about the past. What's done is done. We got business to attend to. Your brother had a ghetto pass that allowed him to operate. The pass is available to you at the same price."

"Man, fuck you and your ghetto pass!

What's past is present motherfucker. You and your dirty ass cops ain't gettin away with what you did to my brother, nigga!"

Ren stepped back and signaled for the guys to move out. "I know you're mad, but think about my offer carefully. I got no problem giving the same deal to the South Side Mexicans and making the PG's my personal whippin boys," Ren stated as he turned and headed for the door with Dwayne watching his back.

"I don't give a damn about no South Siders! Fuck them and you! And get the fuck outta my shop!" Red yelled walking towards Ren and his crew, but he was being restrained by his own subordinates.

"I think we're gonna have trouble with this fucker Ren," Manny commented while walking next to Ren as they headed for the front door.

"Don't worry, the rest of the PG's aren't fools. They'll calm him down and pull his coat about making the right moves. At the end of the day, he'll eventually fall in line once we start putting the squeeze on his entire organization."

"Are you thinking what I'm thinking?" Manny asked.

"You damn right."

They walked back to Ren's car and circled around him while he spoke. "It's time to let this bastard know who he's fucking with! We're going to do a sweep of all PG's business, legal or drug related. If there's one barber in that shop without a license, I want it shut down. Every runner or lookout on the block, I want them picked up. After today, Red and the PG's are going to know who's in control."

CHAPTER 9

Nina pulled up in front of Natalie's house. They had the average home for a cop on a salary. It was three bedroom combination brick and frame house on a small lot. The neighborhood was predominantly white middle class. The only other blacks that lived on the same block were Nina and Ren. Nina had just gotten off work and was going by for her customary visit to check on her friend before she went home. With Keith constantly at work Nina didn't like the fact that Natalie and the kids were by themselves. She could have that baby at any time now. Nina walked up to the front door with her son Michael by her side, rang the bell, and then let herself in.

"Big momma where are you at?"

"I'm in the kitchen girl," Natalie yelled over the rattle of some pots and pans.

"What are you up to in there baby?"

"Whipping up a little dinner, is Michael with you?"

"Yeah."

"Jacob is in the living room watching cartoons," Natalie replied.

Michael walked into the living room and took a seat on the couch next to his buddy Jacob and started watching Sponge Bob with him. Nina let her nose, which smelled the scent of fresh cornbread and smothered pork chops, lead her into the kitchen.

"Natalie you're almost nine months pregnant. You got no business being on your feet cooking a five course meal. You should be resting."

"Yeah I know, but I didn't have anything quick to cook. My momma was supposed to come by and help, but she got called into work."

"Well, here let me help you with that," she said grabbing the cooking utensils and taking over preparing the food.

Natalie took baby steps as she walked over and took a seat at the kitchen table. "So you never told me, but what happened with the special night you planned with Ren the other day?"

"It was great. It was wonderful," Nina replied staring out the window at nothing and tapping her nails on the kitchen counter.

"He didn't spend any time with you did he?" Natalie asked sitting up straight in her chair now. "What really happened?"

Nina turned around and looked at Natalie with a fake smile. "He ah, he couldn't stay. He had to go back to work. He had some paperwork or whatever he had to finish up."

"I bet he did."

"Don't start!"

"C'mon Nina, get your head out the clouds girlfriend. There's gotta be another woman."

"And what if there is? Maybe I'm to blame for it. I have gained a few pounds over the years. And I don't do everything that Ren likes. Maybe you're right. Maybe I need to tighten up on my skills so he won't have to go elsewhere."

"Nina are you listening to yourself? Ren might be fucking around and it's your fault!"

"You don't understand Natalie. I need him and he needs me, even if he don't know it. We're not perfect, but who is?"

"Nina I…" Then all of a sudden Natalie bent over in excruciating pain clutching her stomach with both hands. Closing her eyes and sitting back in her chair, she began taking deep breaths.

"What's wrong?" Nina asked running over and dropping down on one knee.

"I think my water just broke," she replied between breaths.

"Oh shit! Okay, okay, stay calm. I'll call an ambulance."

"No time. It'll be faster if you take me. I got a bag I keep packed by the front door. Call Keith and tell him to meet us at the hospital."

"Alright!" Nina replied as she assisted Natalie to her feet and helped her to the front door. She yelled at the kids to get in the car while she grabbed Natalie's bag. As soon as Nina gets her into her car, she pulled out her cell phone and called Keith.

"Hello."

"Keith this is Nina. Natalie's water broke and we're on our way to the hospital."

"Alright I'm on my way!"

Hanging up the phone quickly, he hopped to his feet with a grin and turned toward the guys. "Natalie's about to have the baby, I gotta get to the hospital!"

"What are you waiting for? Get going we'll follow you," Ren said smiling while rising to his feet and scrambling for his car keys.

***

Nina called ahead to the hospital to inform Natalie's doctor they were on their way. Driving with a swiftness that can almost be considered reckless, she bobbed and weaved through traffic running every red light to make it to the hospital before Natalie could give birth to this child in her car. Natalie was feeling the pain as she dug her nails into the leather seats. She was doing her best to relax but it was no use. The contractions were less than three minutes apart at this point. She just closed her eyes while she was focusing on her breathing techniques. As soon as they pulled in front of St. Paul Hospital, a nurse was waiting out front with a wheel chair to get her directly to labor.

Nina held Natalie's hand from the time they got out of the car, until the time she had to change into her hospital gown. It wasn't really by choice. Natalie had such a tight grip on her hand, that it went pale from lack of circulation.

Keith came busting through the delivery doors just a few minutes after the ladies arrived. With a look on his face like a lost little boy looking for his mom in a department store, he frantically searched for the ladies. As Keith began to question the receptionist for his wife's room number, he spots another nurse wheeling Natalie down the hallway.

"Natalie! Natalie!" Keith blurted out over the silence of the vacant lobby.

"Keith! Wait a second, nurse, that's my husband."

"There's my baby," he yelled out again walking over briskly and taking Natalie's hand from Nina. "You okay baby?"

"Hell nah! I'm in fucking pain!"

"Just try to concentrate on your breathing baby. Remember what we learned in lamaze class," Keith said as he demonstrated the breathing techniques for her. She joined him as the nurse continued to wheel her into the delivery room. The doctor was already there washing up and putting on his gloves.

"Oh my God!" Natalie screamed at the top of her voice. "I need my epidural! I need something for this fucking pain!" She yelled in the direction of the doctor.

THE HANDS OF LOVE · 99

"Okay," the doctor replied as he began to turn Natalie on her side. "I'm sorry, but there can only be one family member allowed in here at a time."

"Oh, okay I was just leaving," Nina said slowly backing out the door.

She went out into the hallway to see Ren standing there. He walked over and gave her a hug and a kiss on the forehead.

"Hey sweetie, how is everything going in there?" Ren asked putting his arm on Nina's shoulder and holding her close. She was shivering from the ice cold waiting room.

"She's gonna be just fine."

"Good, good. You look cold. Want me to get you a cup of coffee. Looks like they just made a fresh batch," Ren observed as he led Nina to a seat right across from a coffee maker.

"That'll be great. You know it kind of gives me that feeling about having another child again. That is until I hear the screams of labor pain," Nina joked shaking her head as she took the cup of coffee from Ren who was sitting between her and Michael.

"I don't know my little buddy here might want a little sister someday. Ain't that right Mike?" Ren turned and started tickling Michael who was in the seat next to him. Michael broke out into laughter as he tried, with no success, to get away from his father's tickling fingers.

A couple of hours went by when Keith came slowly walking out the delivery room.

By then everybody had gotten themselves a cup of coffee and were sitting in the waiting room watching the evening news. Keith and Natalie's parents had arrived and were eagerly waiting to hear a word when they saw him walk out.

"Unbelievable. She is so beautiful," were the words that came out of Keith's mouth as he stood there almost in a trance. He missed the birth of his first child Jacob nine years ago and was determine to be there this time. So the experience of watching his child being born now was overwhelming.

"Can we see her?" His mom asked.

"Yeah she's in the nursery."

Everybody rushed down the hall to the hospital nursery to take a look at the newborn baby. Ren grabbed Keith by the arm and jerked him slightly to break him out of his trance. They followed the rest of them as they pressed their faces against the glass window trying to get a good look at the baby girl.

"So what's her name?" Ren asked Keith.

"Her name is Zakiea. She is eight pounds and six ounces."

"She's beautiful. Congratulations brotha," Ren said as he maneuvered his face against the glass to get a better look.

Keith pulled Ren to the side while everyone else was still fixated on the baby, so that he could speak to him in private. "I thought this would be as good a time as any to ask you this.

You see me and Natalie had talked about this, and we would like you and Nina to be the god parents?"

"Me a godfather? I'd be honored and I know Nina would be too," Ren said as he stepped closer and gave Keith a massive bear hug. "Don't worry son, that little girl of yours is gonna be in great hands."

CHAPTER 10

Captain Riley sat in his office awaiting the arrival of Detective McCain. He was to brief him on the investigation of the Monique Harris case. The Captain heard a knock on his office door and then McCain comes walking through. His suit looked wrinkled like he slept in it all night, as his tie was loosened and the top two buttons of his shirt were undone. His eyes were blood shot red and his breath reeked of coffee.

"Morning Captain," McCain said as he walked in and took a seat.

"Jesus McCain! Have you been here all night?"

"I'm just trying to run down every lead I can before the trail goes cold on me."

"Have you worked up a profile yet?" The Captain asked in that raspy voice of his.

"Yes. I believe he is black, mid to late thirties, professional type with some sort of college education. I also believe he's married with children. He's a man with a stable family life and would have much too lose if his affair became public," McCain answered straightening out his shirt and retying his tie.

"What makes you think he's a married family man?"

"Because her best friend said that Ms. Harris had just ended a secret relationship a couple of months back in which everyone that knew her said that she was visibly shaken over it. A relationship in which Ms. Harris never introduced her best friend to her boy friend. Now, the average woman can't wait to run their mouth about a man they're seeing, especially to a best friend. So for her to keep this boy friend a secret must be because he wanted it that way, which tells me he had something to hide, like a wife."

"What about the best friend? She could have an axe to grind. Maybe the reason she never let her meet him is because she was sleeping with her man. Can you rule this friend out as a suspect?" The Captain asked in sort of a condescending tone.

"I thought about that too. She's single, but there is not one shred of evidence that shows they ever talked. Plus the night of the murder she has a rock solid alibi. She was in the bar getting drunk with her friends when Ms. Harris was killed. I think that's a dead end. My gut tells me it has something to do with this mystery man. We find out who he is, and we'll find the true culprit."

"Okay, continue working that angle and

keep me informed."

Then McCain froze for a second, he sat there staring at the diploma on the Captain's wall. The Captain knows that look. He's seen it before. It's that look of extreme focus, like the light bulb just clicked on in his head.

"What is it?" The Captain asked.

"Do we have access to Forth Worth's police records?"

"No. But we have a liaison officer down-town with a direct pipeline to their offices. Why?"

"I just remembered. A couple of months ago there was a murder in Ft. Worth in which a woman had her hands severed."

"You think it might be related?"

"Women getting their hands chopped off can't be common."

***

McCain met up with Lieutenant Urban Bernstein once he got downtown. Bernstein was the Dallas police office's liaison to the Ft. Worth police department. Since the two cities were side by side, both departments thought that it would be advantageous to have direct lines of communication with each other in the event that cases were related. The position of li-aison was a prestigious one, and Bernstein was milking it for everything its worth. You had the opportunity to rub elbows with some of the most important people in law enforcement including but not limited to the mayor himself. The last man to hold the position made it to Assistant Chief.

"Lieutenant Bernstein, pleasure to meet you sir," McCain said playing nice and giving him his respect even though he had nothing but contempt for the political process.

"How are you doing McCain? Your captain called and said you'll need my assistance," he said offering his hand to be shaken. Bernstein was young around twenty eight. He was a tall brunette with a baby face, yet his demeanor was that of maturity and confidence.

"Yeah, I can use your help with a case I'm working on. About six or seven months ago there was a murder in Ft. Worth involving a woman who had her hands severed. It might be possible that murder could be related to mine. I wonder if you could tell me what you know about it?"

"Sure. Follow me."

Bernstein led McCain to his office and offered him a seat. McCain took a seat in the fine leather chair as he looked around. He noticed the large picture on his wall of an Army jet soaring through the sky with the slogan, "Your attitude determines your altitude". Glancing at Bernstein's modern looking desk, he observed how organized it was. If you look at the average cop's desk they have files and papers everywhere, but not Bernstein. His desk looked like a floor model you might see at Office Max or Staples. He even used a coaster to protect his desk from the can of Coke he was drinking on. Turning on his computer, he started accessing the database. Searching through the files, he finally found the case that McCain was looking for.

"Here we go. The victim's name is Tina Gordon; she's a black thirty-two year old woman who was murdered April 10th. She was found with her hands cutoff in front of her apartment complex. There were no witnesses. Apparently the case stalled out because it was recently transferred to the cold case division."

"Can you pull up the pictures of the crime scene?" McCain asked looking on with great eagerness.

"Yeah, just give me a second," he said as he stroked a couple of keys and up the photographs appeared. "Here take a look." Bernstein repositions the computer monitor so that McCain could take a better look.

McCain studies them and just as he thought the shoes were on the wrong feet. It must have slipped right under the nose of the detectives that were working the case at the time.

"Look there. You see the shoes are on the wrong feet the same as my victim. Do you know if they still have her property?" McCain inquired pointing at the screen.

"Yeah they should."

"What'll it take for me to get a look at it?"

"A phone call," he said with a wink and smile.

Bernstein picked up the phone and called directly to the property room at the downtown police office in Ft. Worth. He jotted down some information and hung up the phone.

"C'mon let's go," Bernstein said taking his sports-coat off the back of the chair he was sitting in and heading for the front door with McCain following closely behind.

***

McCain and Bernstein arrive at the downtown Ft. Worth police plaza within twenty minutes. They entered the building and went down to the bowels of the police station. It was so far down that they had to get out of the elevator and walk down an additional flight of stairs just to reach their destination. This area looked like the paint crew skipped it when they did the rest of the building. Cobwebs were clinging to the fluorescent light fixtures. They flickered as they walked up to the property desk where an over worked corporal came dragging out the backroom. Looking like he was half sleep, he sat down his morning paper on the counter and asked the men very dryly. "What can I do for you fellows?"

"We need to look at the evidence for this case," Bernstein said reaching in his pocket and pulling out a requisition form that he hands to the corporal.

"Give me a minute," the corporal said as he slowly turned and walked down one of the long isles filled with countless boxes of evidence and reappears with a box in seconds.

"You'll have to sign for this," he stated setting the box down in front of them and handing them a clipboard and a pen.

McCain quickly opened the box and found the left shoe. Pulling out the sole, he saw a small piece of paper that was tucked underneath it. He opened it to reveal a neatly typed message, the same message that was under Monique Harris' shoe.

"*The hands that touch me will never touch another.*"

He looked at the corner of the paper to see the number 978.

"Shit! I knew it. I knew they were linked. We got a goddamn serial killer on our hands," McCain stated with a hint of relief and disgust in his voice at the same time. He gathered up all the paperwork and turned towards Bernstein. "Thanks for the help."

"Whoa, whoa, hold up a second. You're going to need my help on this."

"I'm sorry, but I work alone."

"Not on this. Fort Worth has joint jurisdiction on this case. They can easily clear it with downtown to have their personnel assist you with the case. Or even yet, have your case transferred to them since the murder of Tina Gordon predates yours. You need me to keep control of this situation and cut through the red tape."

McCain stood there for a second wearing an exasperated look on his face. "Okay, just remember two things lieutenant. I'm in charge, and stay out of my way."

***

Back at The Ship, Stanton was making his way into Captain Riley's office. He had grown suspicions about the Ghost Squad's actions as they pertain to the Jones case.

"Excuse me Captain, but do you have a minute?" Stanton asked tapping on his cracked door and sticking his head in.

"Yeah, c'mon in," the Captain motioned as his nose was buried deep in a file folder reviewing some information. "So since you've interviewed everyone, your case should be wrapping up?"

"Not quite sir. I need to question Detective Sanders again."

"Well he's on leave right now. His wife just gave birth to a lovely baby girl. But why do you need to question him again anyway? I thought you got all the answers you need already," the Captain inquired looking up for the first time and setting his files on the table.

Stanton bowed his head and scratched the back of his neck. "Something is fishy about these guys' stories Captain. It sounds too contrived, too perfect, almost like it was re-hearsed."

"Maybe their stories sound perfect 'cause that's the way it happened."

"Then explain to me why Detective Sander's fingerprints are on a wall safe in Mr. Jones' house." Stanton pulled a folder from his brief-case and handed it to the Captain. "I had CSU go back and dust the entire house for prints."

He picked up the folder and started thumb-ing through the report. "So what, it means noth-ing. He could've left those prints securing the area."

"Sir, this safe was hidden underneath a pic-ture."

"I don't like what you're implying Stanton."

"I understand sir."

"No you don't," the Captain said sharply. "This department is still mourning from the loss of a good cop. And now you want to open up the wounds and accuse a unit of highly deco-rated cops with impeccable reputations of lying about an investigation involving a convicted drug kingpin and cop killer. Nobody is going to buy that. And frankly nobody cares. The best thing we need now is to move on."

"I know sir. I understand your concerns, but the chief did assign me to this. I'm only doing my job sir."

"Okay. When Sanders gets back from leave, you can question him one more time. But if you don't have anything more tangible than fingerprints on a safe, then this investigation will be over. Understood?" He said with a stoic look on his face.

"Understood Captain."

CHAPTER 11

Ren woke up to the sound of his alarm clock going off. It was six thirty in the morning. An early riser; Ren was up before the alarm even went off. He hit the clock, rolled out of bed, and began his morning routine of getting dress. After a quick shower, he pulled out the Magic Shave, made a thick paste, and put it on his face. He tried conventional shaving only to see his face bump up badly because he had fine hair that would grow under the skin if he cut it too closely. The Magic Shave burned him a little, but it made his face smooth and without the bumps. While the Magic Shave was sitting on his face he went to the closet looking for something to wear. He grabbed a generic gray t-shirt and a customary pair of black stone washed blue jeans. Wiping off the *Magic Shave*, he finished getting dressed. Ren walked into his son's bedroom and woke him up as well. Helping Michael to get dress, Ren heads down stairs to fix them both breakfast. Spending a lot of late hours on the job during the week, Ren tries to make up for it by taking time out in the mornings to get a little one on one with his son. Fixing breakfast for Michael was customary before taking him to school. Nina didn't mind. It let her sleep in.

Ren began to fry up some bacon. He popped some biscuits in the oven and pulled out a second frying pan to cook up some eggs. The aroma crept upstairs, as Michael quickly finished brushing his teeth and ran down stairs to eat. By that time Ren had finished cooking and the food was on the table. Michael sat down licking his lips as he searched for his fork. Ren was an excellent cook, and there was no bigger fan of his cooking then Michael.

"Did you wash your hands?" Ren asked.

"Yes sir," Michael replied picking up his fork ready to dig in.

"Make sure you say your grace first," Ren commands before Michael could get the first bite in his mouth.

"Yes sir. God is grace; God is good, thank you lord for the food about to receive. Amen." Michael said it so fast that it sounded like one word. "Say daddy, you know that baseball sign ups are next Saturday?" Michael asked while stuffing a biscuit in his mouth.

"I know Michael. You've told me about ten times. I'm gonna take you son. Don't worry," Ren said rubbing the top of Michael's head with a smile.

"Are you gonna coach the team again this year?"

"We'll see. Depends on how things go at work. Okay?"

"Okay. 'Cause I was talking to Bobby Wallace the other day. You know my friend that stays in the red house down the street. He said his daddy would coach if you couldn't."

"Hmm, I bet he will. Go ahead and finish eating. Your mom will kill me if you're late for school again."

"Yes daddy."

Michael quickly finished his food and followed his dad through the garage and into the car. Ren pulled out the garage and zipped down the street to the school house. The school wasn't that far away. Matter of fact, most of Michael's friends walk to and from school, but Nina was the over protective type. She didn't like the idea of Michael walking home if she could help it.

"Daddy can you sign my homework planner?" Michael asked pulling out his folder as the car pulled up to the driveway in front of the school.

"Why didn't you get your momma to sign it?"

"I forgot," he said handing Ren the folder acting as if he's in a hurry.

Ren opened it up and signed it. Then the red ink at the top of the page caught his attention. "What's this?"

"Huh?" Michael said with a bewildered look on his face.

"Right here on the top of this page. The teacher wrote down that you've been talking excessively in her class," Ren said locking eyes with Michael. Michael said nothing. He just sat there with his head down.

"Now I see why you didn't have your momma sign this. You know she don't play that, and neither do I," Ren paused for a second, "Look here son. You shouldn't be talking during class. There is plenty of time for that after school. Understand?"

"Yes sir."

"I'm a give you a break this time. I'm a go ahead and sign this, but I better not hear about no more foolishness."

"Yes sir."

"Give me a hug." Ren lean over grabbed him by the back of the head and kissed him on the forehead. "Have a good day at school, and remember what I said, no more foolishness."

"Yes sir. See you later daddy," Michael said as he hopped out the car and sprinted down the sidewalk to the school building entrance. He almost skipped as he was relieved that he didn't get in trouble.

***

Ren got to The Ship just in time for roll call. The rest of the squad was already sitting down with packets in hand waiting for the meeting to begin. Today's roll call seemed a little different.

The tone was much more serious than it normally is. Nobody was laughing or clowning around today. The Captain took the podium with a stone face as the Assistant Chief had come down from headquarters to be by his side. All the seats were taken so Ren just stood against the wall next to a couple of uniform cops.

"Ladies and gentlemen we have had some new and unfortunate developments in the Harris case. It appears that her murder is connected to another murder in Fort Worth. Ms. Tina Gordon on April 10th was killed and had her hands severed in the exact same fashion as Ms. Harris. They both had the same message left in their shoes, and I quote, "The hands that touch me will never touch another." It's apparent that we're dealing with a serial killer. We don't know if there are any others yet. As of right now, this case has become the number one priority of this department. All resources will be used to further this investigation. We will be working with the Fort Worth police department in a joint investigation that will continue to be headed by Detective McCain. Please look over you packet closely. That's all." The Captain closed his file of papers and walked away from the podium with his head down and a somber look on his face.

The room cleared quickly as everyone returned to their desk and talked among themselves over the information that was just given to them. Ren followed his guys into the club house. Walking over to his locker he took a seat facing it. He was still staring at the pictures of the two murdered women that were in his packet with a blank expression on his face.

Keith was the last guy to walk in closing the club house door behind him.

"Here's our boy!" Manny yelled out with a smile.

"Hey, how was that week off?" Dwayne asked coming over to give him some dap along with Manny and Jason.

"A lot of sleepless nights," Keith joked.

"You had quite a shindig Sunday. That christening was all that," Manny said.

"Thanks. I appreciate all you guys coming," Keith replied as he walked over behind Ren and tapping him on his shoulders, "Especially the Godfather here."

"It was an honor," Ren said as he turned around and faced Keith with the same blank expression on his face.

Then the door to the clubhouse opened. "Excuse me Detective Sanders," Stanton interjected with a quarter smile on his face, "I need to have a word with you. It'll only take a minute."

"Sure," Keith replied as he followed Stanton out the clubhouse and into the lobby.

Ren went back to staring at the pictures, as he sort of fell into a trance. Manny and Dwayne were sitting at the table going over their notes.

No one else was paying much attention, except Jason. He saw what happened and walked to the door to see Keith and Stanton going into the Captain's office. He walked back in the club house and closed the door.

"Ren did you see that?" Jason asked walking over to his locker. Ren was still sitting there with the same blank expression staring at those photos. He didn't acknowledge Jason at first.

"Ren!" Jason shouted snapping his fingers.

"What?"

"You okay?"

"Yeah, yeah. I'm fine. What were you saying now?"

"It's Stanton. He came and got Keith to ask him some more questions." Jason walked back to the cracked door with his eyes fixed on the Captain's office.

"So what," Ren responded shrugging his shoulders. "It's probably nothing. Stanton is just closing all the loose ends."

"I don't like it. I just don't like it. Why ain't he asking any of us extra questions?"

"Keith is a stand up guy. There is nothing to worry about." Ren stood up, put his gun in his holster, and closed his locker. A uniform cop knocked on the door. "Detective Love, you have a young lady out here to see you sir."

"Okay," Ren walked to the door and put his arm around Jason's shoulder. "Don't worry."

Ren strolled out to the floor to see Samantha. Samantha was Ren's long time paid confidential informant, otherwise known as a snitch. Ren first met her when he busted her pimp five years ago. Back then, Samantha was a sixteen year old runaway from Kansas with two baby boys and no idea of who their fathers were. She was strung out on crystal-meth at the time and living in cheesy motels. Ren felt sorry for her and even more so for her two little boys. So he helped get her a one bedroom apartment and put her on the payroll as a C.I. Samantha's photographic memory and the fact that she came to know a lot of the criminal underground through her former pimp's contacts, made her an asset.

Samantha was sitting at a desk chugging down a Coke and nervously scratching her head. She was wearing a ragged looking flower print dress. Her hair looked like she hadn't had a perm in over a year. Her nails were in desperate need of a manicure. Yet she still was a good looking woman, all things considered. She had an hourglass figure and sandy red skin. Though she looked rough looking, she had a pair of the prettiest brown eyes that if you stared directly into them, you would buy anything that she was selling.

"Hey Ren," she said in a soft voice. So soft, that Ren leaned closer because if he didn't, he couldn't hear her talk.

"What's up?"

"I need to talk to you. You got a minute."

"Sure. Step over here."

She followed Ren into a secluded hallway.

He turned around and leaned against the wall. "What you got for me?"

"It's Red. He's mad. You've been really hurting his businesses with all these raids. He's been talking some crazy shit lately."

"Oh yeah. Like what?"

"Well, ah, he's saying shit like he wants to get even with you for killing his brother. That he's going to make you pay."

"Yeah, I already know all about that. You come down here to tell me this?" Ren said feeling a bit agitated.

"Well, ah, I was hoping that would be worth a little something."

"Didn't I just give you a hundred last week?"

"Yeah, but I need some more money for a baby sitter. I gotta go to my AA meetings."

"Samantha cut the shit. We both know that you're not going to any damn meetings. What happened?"

"The, ah, the lights got cut off yesterday."

"If I've told you once, I've told you a thousand times," Ren snapped furiously. He reached into his pocket and pulled out his wallet. He grabbed two hundred dollar-bills and handed it to her. "This is the last fucking time Samantha! I'll be by your place Friday. The lights better be on and there better be food in the kitchen for them boys or I swear to God I'll call child protective services myself. Understand?" He barked waving his index finger in her face.

"Yes. Thank you so much Ren. I don't know what I'd do without you," she sniffled lowering her head in shame. "You know I would love to show you my real appreciation," she gently reached for his hand.

Ren pulled away from her advance. "Don't start that shit! And don't even think about shedding those crocodile tears. Get your ass home and get those lights on, now."

Ren turned and left in disgust. He headed back into the clubhouse where the guys were sitting at the table with their feet up watching television. "What's on the tube?" Ren asked as walked over to his locker to grab a few more things.

"Oprah," Manny replied.

"Oprah!" Ren snickered. "What's next? Are you ladies gonna start discussing your feelings over tea and crumpets?"

"It's not even like that Ren. We were just flipping through the channels and came across this interview she's having with a man that got pregnant," Dwayne interjected.

"Bullshit!" Ren said.

"He's serious. It's some weird shit about some man that use to be a woman, or had a sex change or something. And his wife some kind of way got him pregnant."

Ren walked over and took a look at the interview Oprah was having, "A man having a baby, huh? Just the thought of that makes my dick softer than wet tissue," Ren commented as the boys broke out in laughter. "Well, back to business. Dwayne and Manny I want you two to get over to South Sider territory and try to get a feeling on what they think about the new change in leadership with the PG's. Jason, as soon as Keith gets finished with Stanton, I want you two to sit on Red. I wanna know what he's got cooking. I'll check in with you later," Ren commanded.

***

Keith stepped in the Captain's office behind Stanton and took a seat. "So what can I help you with?"

Stanton walked around in front of the desk and sat on the edge. "I just had a couple of additional questions I needed to ask you to tie up some loose ends before I close the investigation."

"Sure. Whatever I can do to help."

"Great! Now you said the first time we talked that you and Manny entered through the rear door and once shots were fired you guys secured the area, right?"

"Right!"

"After that, did you do any further search of the home?" Stanton stood up and began pacing back and forth.

"Just a visual search of everything that was in plain view. The drugs were sitting on the couch. Once we checked Mr. Jones' vital signs and saw that he was dead, we called the coroner and CSU to take over the crime scene," Keith answered readjusting himself in his seat.

"So you didn't search any other areas of the home?"

"That's correct."

"Maybe you can tell me why your finger-prints are on a wall safe?"

"Ah, I'm not sure I follow you?"

"CSU dusted the entire house for prints and found yours on a wall safe that was covered with a picture," Stanton said handing a copy of the report to Keith. Keith opened it up and scan through the report. His facial expression went from one of indifference to concern within seconds.

"I must've accidentally touched it when securing the area."

"How are you going to accidentally touch a safe concealed by a picture?"

"Just what are you implying?"

"I'm not implying anything. I'm stating facts. And here's another one. The safe was empty," Stanton said sarcastically.

Keith just sat there for a minute. He cut his eyes at Stanton. "I'm not answering any more questions without my union rep."

"What's wrong?" Stanton asked with raised eyebrows.

"I don't like where this line of questioning is going."

"Is it because you guys are not shooting me

straight about what really happened that morning," he paused for a second. "You don't strike me as the conniving, underhanded type. Maybe you just got caught up in something bigger than what you could control. If you cooperate with me now your career might not be in jeopardy."

Keith didn't say anything else. He just nervously started rubbing his mustache.

Stanton curled his thin lips into a sinister looking grin. He smelled blood in the water. Squatting down to one knee, he is now eye to eye with Keith. Lowering his voice, he tried to be as sympathetic as possible. "Do you really want a full scale investigation into every aspect of this case? Do you have any idea of the power I have? Do you know what I can do? I can put your entire life under a microscope. With one phone call I can get a subpoena to pull your credit card statements, bank account statements, and check all your deposits."

Keith hung his head low sinking into his chair.

"I see from your file that you're married with a son. And I heard that your wife just gave birth to a brand new baby girl. Congratulations," Stanton said continuing to pace back and forth. "You think your family will be proud of your actions? What do you think their reaction is going to be when we show up at your home with a search warrant and turn your place upside down? I also hear that you're a devout Catholic, and that you attend mass every Sunday. I wonder what your priest will think when he finds out that you were lying and withholding information. Do yourself a favor, save your family the embarrassment. Do the right thing while you still can, and tell me everything that happened?"

Keith looked up at Stanton with puppy dog eyes. Rubbing his hands together, Keith nervously cracked his knuckles. In a cracked voice he slowly starts to speak. "I should have never…"

"Should have never what?" Stanton asked on the edge of his seat. He knew that Keith was on the verge of possibly breaking. That with the right motivation Keith would spill his guts from the guilt. His instincts were right. He knew he leaned on the right guy.

Then there was a knock at the door and it cracked open. "Is Captain Riley in here?" It was Jason sticking his head in through the door. Jason knew the Captain wasn't in there, but he had grown suspicious.

"No!" Stanton snapped with a cold hard stare. "Do you mind, we're in the middle of something?"

"Oh, I'm sorry to interrupt," Jason said pretending to be shocked. "You okay Keith?"

Keith in that split second was able to regain his composure. He rose to his feet. "Yeah I'm straight." He threw on a fake smile and turned toward Stanton. "Well, I gotta get back to work. I like having these kinda debates. And no matter what you say, I still think Tyson would've beaten Ali in their prime. I'm glad we were able to tighten up those loose ends too."

"Oh, okay," Stanton said smiling and playing along with Keith.

Keith casually followed Jason out closing the door behind him. Jason was even more suspicious by what transpired. As they walked thru the halls Jason turned back toward Keith.

"The rest of the guys already took off. Ren wants us to sit on Red's place. So we better get going."

"Sure. I just need to go to the head right quick. Give me a minute."

Keith went into the men's room and stood over the sink. He ran some cold water, took a hand full, and splashed it on his face. He looked at the mirror and didn't like the reflection that was staring back at him. Stanton was the first person that Keith ran into that questioned his character since he's been on the force. Something that Keith has always taken pride in. He's always been a very spiritual man, and the fact that he has taken part in some questionable things since joining the Ghost Squad is hurting him to his soul. He was faced with a precarious dilemma. Be a stand up guy and stay loyal to his squad, or come clean about everything and get the peace of mind that comes with it.

***

Ren looked at his watch and realized he was running late for his ten o'clock appointment. He flew through traffic like a mad man and pulled into the driveway of the Lutheran Memorial Hospice at about five after. Don't be fooled by the name. The Lutheran Memorial Hospice was not some super large medical facility. It was a small five bedroom house in the middle of a residential neighborhood. The name wasn't even on the front, for the privacy of some patients. It is for people that are in need of end of life care. About ninety five percent of the people who enter the facility die. It's a place that offers a family environment with around the clock supervision. The patients are all treated with dignity and respect. Right now the house was full to capacity.

Ren finally arrived. He rushed through the living room, down the hall, and made it just in time to see the doctor exiting his father's room. "Dr. Taylor," Ren said in between gasps of breath. "Looks like I caught you just in time."

"Mr. Love, how are you doing?"

"Good. I just got held up at the job. Sorry I'm late."

"Quite alright, I just finished looking in on your father," Dr. Taylor said shaking Ren's hand.

"How's he doing Doc?"

Dr. Taylor looked back to make sure that Ren's father couldn't hear them talk. He leaned closer. "Not too good. The Congestive heart failure is starting to take its toll on his body. His heart is getting larger and his body is retaining too much fluid. We're about to pass the point of no return. If he doesn't get a heart transplant, and I mean soon, there'll be nothing more we can do for him other than make him comfortable."

"How soon can you get his name on the transplant list?"

"As I told you before, since your father has no health insurance, you have to show in good faith the financial ability to pay for the operation. And a heart transplant along with the follow up care is going to run about in the two hundred thousand dollar range."

"Yeah I know," Ren said exhaling. "I'm working on that. I should have the money by the end of the month."

"I'll be waiting to hear from you. I got to go. I have another appointment. I'll be by to check on your father later this week."

"Thanks for everything Doc."

"No problem."

Ren walked in the room to see his father resting comfortably. Morgan Love, a sixty seven year old retired salesman, was the only parent that Ren had left in this world. His mother had left them when Ren was eight years old. She went to the store one morning for cereal and never came back. His father continued to raise him on his own and never remarried. About two years ago he was diagnosed with

Congestive Heart Failure. As his health began to fade, Ren had his father move in with him so that he could take care of him. But once his father became completely bed ridden, the task of taking care of him was too much for Ren and Nina to handle alone. So they were force to put him in a hospice.

Ren approached the old man's bed and gently grabbed his hand. "How are you doing pop?"

His father opened his eyes and smiled. Ren was the spitting image of his father. The only difference was the wrinkles and grey hair. He used what seems like every bit of energy he had to sit up. He struggled to get the words out his mouth. "I'm fine son."

"I talked to the doctor. He said you're improving," Ren lied sitting down on the stool next to the bed.

"You know it's not a good thing to lie to a dying man."

"C'mon pop, you gotta keep a positive outlook. I'm gonna have the money for you to get on that donor's list by the end of this week."

"I appreciate what you're trying to do son. But like I told you when I first moved in this place, I came here to die."

"Dad you gotta stop talking like that," Ren said rolling his eyes.

"Look here son. I've lived a long and fulfilling life. You've been a great son, and you've given me a great grandson. That's more than any man can ask for. I'm ready." His strength gave way, and he sunk back down in bed.

"Do me a favor, stop the dying talk. We need you around a little bit longer. So try to relax and save your strength. Look here, I brought your favorite." Ren reached into the paper bag he was holding and pulled out a pint of Dutch chocolate ice cream and a plastic spoon. "Here, let me help you sit up," Ren said readjusting the pillows behind him so that he could feed him properly. Taking the top off the pint, he began feeding his father small amounts of ice cream. Since it melted a little on the way over, it was easy for the old man to swallow it.

After his father ate about half the pint, Ren wiped his father's face and stood up. "Now I gotta get back to work, so I'll check in with you later on. Please try to take it easy," he said kissing his father on the forehead before rushing out the door.

CHAPTER 12

Cynthia was devastatingly beautiful this evening. Her hair was fierce. The low cut, gray, silk, dress she wore was breathtaking. It clinged to her soft bronze skin in all the right places. Barely coming pass her thighs, the short dress showed off those lavish legs of hers. Sitting on the edge of the couch at her friend's get-together holding a paper plate of finger food, she flirted with the eligible bachelor that was next to her. She didn't have to try to hard though, because his eyes were fixated on her cleavage the entire time. Encouraging his behavior, Cynthia laughed at all his jokes while patting him on the knee.

"So, we've been talking all this time and I never caught your name," he asked.

"My name is Cynthia, but my friends call me Cindy," she answered grinning ear to ear.

"Nice to formally meet you Cindy, my name is Carl. So ah, how do you know Bobby?" Carl asked taking a sip of his beer. The living room was a little warm so Carl peeled off his sports coat and put it on the arm of the couch.

"Bobby is my girl. We go way back. We've been working together for over ten years. And before that, we both did our internships at UT Southwest."

"Oh, okay, so you work at Methodist Hospital too?"

"Yeah, I'm a registered nurse."

"Professional woman, I see you girl," he joked. 'What college did you attend?"

"Texas Southern of course," Cynthia boasted. "And you?"

"I went to Prairie View. I got my masters in computer science."

"So did you pledge while you were down there?"

"Definitely, I'm a Que," he bragged proudly pulling up the sleeve on his shirt to reveal the large Que that was branded on his bicep. "What about you?"

"I belong to the best sorority there is, AKA."

Interrupting their conversation was the host of the party and Cynthia's friend Bobby, who was setting up the card table in the middle of the room. "Okay everybody it's time!" She announced motioning with her hand for the rest of her guests to join her in the living room. "For those of you who don't know how to play *Taboo* listen up while I explain," Bobby said putting the game on the table and pulling out all the accessories. "All you have to do is get your team to say the name on the card without saying the banned words or using your hands in the time allotted. If you break the rules the person monitoring you on the other team can buzz you," she explained putting two chairs under the card table, "Everybody got it?"

The mixed crowd of couples and a few singles nodded their heads in agreement. They all begin pilling into the living room bringing with them extra chairs.

"Let's separate into teams. Men versus the women," Bobby said rubbing her hands together in delight.

Cynthia and Carl ignored everyone else as they were still wrapped up in their own private world. As Cynthia sat there with her lovely legs crossed taking small bites of the chicken wings that Bobby was serving, she felt a sharp pain in her stomach.

"Excuse me Carl. I'll be back in a minute," she said rising quickly to her feet. She immediately headed for the kitchen where another one of her friends, Janet, was standing.

"Janet!"

"What's up girl? I see you've met Carl."

"Yes child, that man has a chest that made my knees get weak. Good thing I was sitting down."

"Girl you so crazy."

"But look here, I got to run home right quick. Tell Bobby I'll be back if she asks."

"What's wrong? You just got here."

"I got to use the bathroom girl."

Janet took a couple of steps back and glanced down the hallway. "Nobody is in the bathroom. You can go ahead."

"No, I don't think you understand. I got to launch a missile."

"So! What's wrong with Bobby's bathroom?"

"I can't use the bathroom in a house full of people. It just won't come out. Besides, I'm real particular about where I boo boo, okay," Cynthia whispered intensely while her head was on a swivel making sure no one else could hear. "So I'll be right back. Just do me a favor, keep these bitches away from Carl."

Once outside, Cynthia walked briskly towards her car while whipping out her keys. As she got in she happened to see another car down the street with its lights on and the engine running. Thinking nothing of it, she quickly threw the car in gear and jetted down the street towards her house. Clutching her stomach, she maneuvered her way through traffic to the sound of Mary J. Blige playing in the background. The leather seats in her luxurious BMW could offer no comfort as the pain in her stomach increased with every mile she drove.

Cynthia pulled up to her condo in the prestigious West Village area. West Village is known for its great location being in close proximity to downtown. It has some of the best restaurants, coffee bars, and shopping in the city. Normally a neighborhood buzzing with people,

but on this hot summer night it was uncharac-
teristically deserted. In a rush to use the bathroom and get back to the party, she decided to
park on the street in front of her place instead of
the parking garage. While putting her car in
park, she noticed a car pulling up directly behind her. The lights were similar to the car she
saw at Bobby's place. Turning off the engine
she grabbed her purse from the passenger seat
and got out of the car. She could also hear the
car door slamming from the vehicle behind her.
Stepping up on the curb she walked down the
long side walk towards her condo. As she made
her way to her front door she heard the footsteps of someone walking behind her. Coming
to an abrupt stop, she turned around quickly and
yelled, "Whose there?"

"It's me."

Cynthia didn't quite recognize the voice as
she struggled to see the person approaching her.
Dressed in all black she couldn't make out anything including the face until the person was
right up on her.

"Oh it's you," Cynthia sighed. "What are
you doing here? Did you, did you follow me?"

"I needed to see you."

"See me, for what? I thought we were
through."

"I just needed to show you something."

"What!"

The individual cleverly approached her
avoiding any direct light. The black clothes and

lateness of the hour concealed her pursuer's true motives as a long sharp blade was slyly hidden behind their back. The person calmly approached making Cynthia feel more comfortable causing her to drop her guards for a second. With each step they got closer and closer while Cynthia was fumbling through her keys to find the one that would open her front door. As she finally found it, she looked up to see that they were eye to eye. Cynthia gasped in horror and her body became immediately paralyzed with fear at the sight of a sharp blade the stranger whipped out. She opened her mouth to scream, but before she could make a sound, the blade had slit her slender throat with a vengeance. Falling to the ground in excruciating pain, she held her throat trying to stop the bleeding.

"Why?" She struggled to say.

The person came over, grabbed her by the hair, and leaned in close. "Because the hands that touch me will never touch another!" Then the mysterious figure slashed the back of her neck with great force.

CHAPTER 13

McCain and Bernstein pulled up to the Ft. Worth home of Gale Gordon. Gale was the mother of Tina Gordon, one of the young ladies that had been brutally murdered. They walked up the front porch to the sound of wind chimes being blown by the gentle breeze. McCain pulled back the screen and knocked on the door of the small frame house. The door opened but the chain lock was still on so that you could only see her face through the crack of the door.

"Who is it?" An old lady asked fixing her glasses on her face.

"It's the police Ma'am. We're looking for a Gale Gordon.?" McCain said as both men whipped out their badges and held them up so that she could see them.

"Just a minute," she said as she closed the door back, took off the chain, and then she re-opened the door with one hand clinched to her floral house coat. "C'mon in and have a seat."

They strolled in her place as she offered

them a seat on her plastic covered loveseat. The strong scent of mothballs circulated through the air. Her house was cramped as the men's knees rubbed up against the coffee table while they took a seat on the couch.

"I'm Gale what can I help you with?" She asked taking a seat in her rocking chair across from them.

"My name is Detective McCain and this is Lieutenant Bernstein. There has been some new information that's turned up in the death of your daughter, Tina. We like to ask you a few questions."

"I know. It's all in the papers," she replied pointing to a copy of the Dallas Times which was sitting on the coffee table. It had on the front page in large three inch headlines, "TWO BRUTAL MURDERS ARE CONNECTED." Gale leaned back in her rocking chair and grabbed some tissue from the Kleenex box next to her on the table as a tear began falling down her face. "Tina was my only child. She was a beautiful young lady that died too soon, and no one seemed to care but me." Gale picked up a photo album that was next to her and pulled out a picture of Tina. She handed it to McCain who stared at it for a moment before handing it to Bernstein.

"I'm sorry ma'am, I know this investigation in the past hasn't been properly handled, but now it has the full attention of the police department. We're going to do everything possible to catch this killer."

"It only took another woman dying first."

"I understand how you feel, but if you want your daughter's killer brought to justice, we're going to need your cooperation."

She continued to dab her eyes with tissue. "Okay."

"Good," McCain said pulling his notepad out of his suit pocket. "Now was Tina seeing anyone before she passed away?"

"Not anything serious as far as I could tell."

"Are you sure? I mean can you recall anyone that she might have casually went out with?"

"Now that you mention it, I do remember a guy she went out with almost a year ago. You see Tina, whenever she went out on a first date; she always had the guy meet her in a neutral spot. She would never let a guy know where she lived until he *passed the test* as she referred to it. It just so happened that one Saturday afternoon she had a date and this guy was supposed to pick her up at Starbucks where we were having a cup of coffee. He pulled up in a blue Mustang. He got out for a second. As soon as she saw him, she kissed me goodbye and hopped in his car. She never did let me meet him. It was like it was some big damn secret. I kinda got the impression that the man was married or something."

McCain and Bernstein turned and looked at each other. "Did you get a good look at this guy?" McCain inquired further jotting down all the information.

"Yes."

"You think you would recognize him if you saw him again?"

"I'm bad with names, but I never forget a face. Why? You think he may have had something to do with her death?"

"It's possible. Can you come with us? We need you to look at a few photos as soon as possible."

"Sure. Just let me change first." Gale walked into the backroom to change.

"So what are you thinking?" Bernstein asked McCain.

"It sounds to me like the same M.O, both women having affairs with a married man. It's no coincidence. These killings are definitely linked to our mystery man."

"You think she'll really be able to ID a man she only saw once, almost a year ago, for a few seconds?" Bernstein questioned with a raised eyebrow.

"Maybe, anything is possible. But no matter what, I think we just got our first breakthrough, especially if she can give us an ID."

***

McCain and Bernstein returned to The Ship after spending all day downtown with Gale Gordon looking at countless photos. She never saw anyone that came close to resembling the man that she saw in front of Starbucks. So McCain had her describe the suspect to a sketch artist for a composite drawing. Having a squad car take the old lady back home, they immediately made their way back to The Ship to update Captain Riley on their progress and show him the sketch. Upon their arrival, McCain went straight to the Captain's office and tapped on the door.

"Come on in. What you got?" The Captain asked.

"It looks like our ladies were dating the same guy, a married man who was very secretive about his affairs. The mother of Ms. Gordon saw him and the car he was driving. She says that she can positively identify him. We showed her a photo array, but apparently he hasn't been in the system. So we had a sketch made." McCain hands the sketch to him.

Captain Riley looked at the sketch it seemed from every angle. "Why does this guy look familiar?"

"I said the same thing the first time I looked at it too," McCain retorted while scratching his head.

"Okay, I want you to call my friend with the FBI. Have them work up a new profile based on all the information you're giving me, and go back to that apartment complex and see if they have any video surveillance. Maybe your guy or his car was caught on tape. Circulate that sketch too. Maybe somebody else has spotted this guy."

"I'm on it."

Then the phone rang on the Captain's desk. He picked it up and listened while nodding his head at the same time. McCain and Bernstein started to walk out of the office when the Captain motioned for them to holdup. He grabbed a pad of paper and began to jot something down.

"I got some more bad news. It looks like we got another body." He handed McCain the piece of paper with the address written down on it. "It looks like the same M.O. Get down there right away and see if it's our guy that's responsible."

"Yes sir."

***

They arrive at the scene around two in the afternoon. The sun was out, and it was cooking anyone standing directly in it. McKinney Ave. which ran through the heart of West Village was the scene of this latest crime. The luxury condos and apartments that made up this exclusive neighborhood was a buzz with residents in the streets being nosey trying to see what happen. The uniform cops had already put up the yellow tape and secured the area. McCain turned on his siren and drove through the police barricades. He slowly got out the car, put on his dark shades he likes to wear in the summer, and flashed his detective badge to the officer in charge.

"I'm Detective McCain and this is Lieutenant Bernstein."

"Right this way gentlemen. The body is over here," the Sergeant said escorting them across the parking lot to the crime scene.

"Do you have an ID on the victim Sergeant?"

"Yes sir." He flipped out a notepad and began to read from it. "Her name is Cynthia Morrow. She is a thirty year old African American, single female, who's been living in this building for about three years."

"Did she have a purse or anything at the scene?"

"No. Apparently she was killed right before she could enter into her own front door. The neighbors, who called it in, gave us her information."

"Good job Sergeant."

McCain pulled out two sets of latex gloves and gave a pair to Bernstein. They could smell the foul odor of death as they walked up the sidewalk to see the blood drench body lying only inches from the front door of her condo. McCain looked around to see if he could spot any obvious clues. Anything that would stand-out immediately, but at first glance nothing seems out of place. Standing over the body was the Medical Examiner, who was already there as usual.

"Joan, do you ever sleep?"

She stands up and turns around. "I should be

asking you that same question."

"I sleep in between cases," McCain joked. "So what do we got here?"

"The victim had her throat slashed. See," Joan explained pointing to her neck where the injuries had occurred. "You see the depth and length of the cut. It's almost identical to the previous victims. I got no doubt that the same weapon was used on all three victims."

"The same M.O," McCain said rubbing his chin. "I guess we got one more thing to do to make it official."

McCain kneels down with Bernstein looking on. Carefully sliding off her shoe, he saw a piece of paper tucked in the sole. Pulling out the paper he unfolds the paper to reveal that familiar message. Typed in that eerie manner were the words that would continue to make everyone tense, and instill fear throughout the city.

"*The hands that touch me will never touch another.*"

In the corner of the paper was another set of numbers 007. He hands it to Bernstein, who had this inquisitive look on his face as he examined the paper closely. McCain opened his briefcase and pulled out a copy of the sketch and a description of the car.

"Sergeant!"

"Yes sir."

"This is our guy. The Ship is taking this case. I want a canvas of the neighborhood. Let's say about a three mile perimeter. I want you to circulate this sketch and vehicle description," McCain instructed as he handed the Sergeant the information.

"We'll get right on it."

"What the hell do these numbers mean?" Bernstein asked McCain as his eyes were glued to the note.

"I don't know. But I tell you what. I've been on the force for thirty years now, and I've worked a ton of cases and I've seen a lot of strange things, but none as strange as this. I'm still convinced that our mystery man is behind this."

CHAPTER 14

After a long day on the job, Ren was ready to head home. He walked out The Ship and was getting in his car when the phone rang. Not his normal cell phone, but another prepaid phone that he uses for *Special Calls*.

"Yeah," he answered sharply in his customary way.

"Hey baby it's me, Heather," she said in a sexy voice.

"I'm glad you called."

"Nice to know I'm being thought of. I wanna see you tonight. Why don't you come on by?"

"Where are you at?"

"I'm at our spot."

"I'll be there in about ten minutes. I got something important I need to talk to you about."

Ren hung up the phone and hopped in his car. He swiftly drove to the Howard Johnson Hotel and pulled right up to the front door. The hotel was just off the freeway. Being that it's a week night, the place was empty. Heather always reserved the same room, 456. Before his fist could hit the door for the second knock, she swung the door open. She was standing there in a sexy sheer night gown. She licked her lips and struck a sexy pose.

"You ready for this daddy?"

"Always! But I need to talk to you first," he responded walking through he door with a serious look on his face.

"Too much talking kills my mood Ren. Look here, I've been drinking shots of gin, my nipples are hard, and I'm already moist and ready. Please don't make me wait," Heather stressed getting on the bed on all fours.

"It's important," Ren said gesturing for her to have a seat.

"Fine! What's so damn important?" Heather climbed off the bed and took a seat in the arm chair across from Ren with her arms folded in disgust.

"Look here; have you seen anyone following you lately? You know a stranger that might look outta place or something."

"No not really."

"What about your husband?"

"I thought you never wanted me to bring him up."

"I don't, but what if he knows about us?"

"He doesn't know shit! He spends all of time working on cases, even when he's at home."

"Working on cases?"

"Yeah, he's a cop. And ever since he took this new Internal Affairs job, that he can't stop talking about, he doesn't have time for anything else, including me."

"Your husband is a cop and you didn't think that bit of information was important?"

"First of all it was your idea to keep our personal lives secret. I don't ask you about your wife, and you don't ask me about my husband, remember? Next, you guys don't even work in the same building. He works downtown."

Ren tried to stay patient as he slowly murmured the words, "What is your husband's name?"

"Greg Stanton," she said rolling her eyes.

"Oh shit!" Ren murmured under his breath. He closed his eyes and tilted his head toward the ceiling.

"What's wrong?" She asked sitting back against some pillows she propped up on the headboard.

Ren debated in his head if he should mention the situation at The Ship with Stanton, that keen mind of his started running through all the different scenarios in an instant. He couldn't afford to piss off Heather or make her paranoid. He needed to keep her trust for the time being. "Nothing is wrong baby. It's just been a long day. We've been working this case. You probably heard of it, the *Hands off Killings*."

"Vaguely, I haven't really been keeping up

with the news lately. Didn't they find two women with their hands chopped off or something like that?"

"That's right. Some psychopath is on the loose and the whole case has me a little on edge. And I'm a little concern about you, that's all."

"That is so sweet Ren. Your presence makes me feel safe already. Matter of fact, just the thought of you worrying about me makes me feel all warm inside. Why don't you feel for yourself?" She took Ren's hand and placed it on her c-cup size chest. The rhythm of her heartbeat quicken with his touch. With eyes closed, she moved closer as their lips found each others and they begin to slowly kiss. She allowed her tongue to glide down Ren's thick chocolate neck. Her soft touch is just what Ren needed after a long stressful day. He knew he had to get home, and that Nina was waiting on him. But he could no longer fight off Heather's advances. Determine, she pulled off his shirt and unbuckled his belt in a seductive fashion as her nails slid gently down his chest. He fell back on the bed as she continued to kiss him from head to toe and cleverly taking his pants off at the same time. She reached for a small bag on the nightstand that contained a can of whip cream and a box of cherries. Ren's eyes grew wider and his dick got harder as she approached taking the top off the can of whip cream and placing the cherries on the bed. She drew lines of whip cream on Ren's chest then put the cherries on it and slowly twirled them around. Next, she straddled him not letting him enter her yet, as she had another trick up her sleeve. She would pickup a whip cream covered cherry and place it on his lips. And just before he could take a bite, she quickly pulled it back seductively teasing him. Then she would take the cherry and put it next to her nipple. Ren would place both in his mouth simultaneously. He grabbed her by the waist and flipped her over so that now he's on top, just like he likes it.

"Now that's what I'm talking about daddy," she said grinning.

"Oh I know. I know this is what you been wanting." Ren took her in his arms once again and made love to her.

***

After about an hour of intense sex, Ren finally made his way home. He pulled in the driveway at ten o'clock at night. The light was still on in the kitchen and he could see Nina at the sink doing dishes. Walking in the door, he sat his gun and badge on the table and took a seat on the couch.

"Hey baby," he said to Nina who walked in the living room after hearing him come through the garage door.

"Long day at work?" She asked walking

over and giving him a kiss.

"Yeah."

"I cooked dinner. I got some fried chicken, mashed potatoes, and macaroni and cheese. You want me to warm you up a plate?"

"Sure, it sounds good," Ren said kicking his shoes off and propping his feet up on the coffee table. Lifting up the seat cushions, he searched for the remote control so he could turn on the evening news.

Nina went into the kitchen and popped a plate she had already fixed for Ren earlier into the microwave. She grabbed a TV tray and placed his plate on it, and then set it in front of him.

"Thanks baby," Ren said rubbing his hands before diving into the food.

"So you wanna tell me about your day?" She asked staring at Ren enjoying the food she'd prepared for him.

"Same ole shit, just a lot of cases that need my attention. What about you? How was your day?"

"I've been having problems at work with this chick who's my new supervisor. Ever since she took over, Mrs. Thang has been hating on me. I think it's probably 'cause her fat ass has hair that's this long." She snapped her fingers.

"I think you're over reacting," Ren said shoving another spoon full of potatoes in his mouth.

"Nah baby, she's been giving me more files

to do than anyone else. She comes by my desk twice as much as everyone else. I'm telling you this bitch is out to get me."

"Baby please! It's not as serious as you're making it out to be. This ain't the set of *Dynasty* or *General Hospital*. You work in a call center for an insurance company."

Nina rolled her eyes, folded her arms, and sat back on the couch. Ren noticed the look on her face and dropped his fork. He wiped off his hands and scooted the tray out of the way.

"Put'em up here," he commanded patting his lap for Nina to prop her feet up. She just sat there. Ren reached over and took off her shoes and place her feet in his lap. Firmly, he began to massage her sore feet.

"I'm sorry baby. I didn't mean to make light of your job. I know you've had a long day," he said making a circular motion with his thumb on the ball of foot.

"Ooh that feels good! Thank you baby," she said lying back on the couch with both feet in his lap now. "Say why don't we go up stairs? Michael is asleep. We got the whole place to ourselves. I'll give you a special treat," she joked grabbing one of his hands rubbing it against her face.

"I love to baby, but not now. I'm really tired."

She moved closer and looked under his chin. She noticed that Ren had recently shaved and he had a number of ingrown hairs that were turning into small bumps, despite the fact that he used the Magic Shave. She opened a small box on the end table and pulled out a sewing needle.

"Tilt your head back," Nina commanded.

Ren gladly rested his head back on the couch and Nina got closer and began to gently use the needle to pick the ingrown hairs out of his skin. This was one of the weapons she used at her disposal to get her way. She enjoyed pampering Ren, and he enjoyed being pampered.

"C'mon upstairs and let me love on you baby."

"I would. You know I would. But I'm really exhausted baby. I got no strength right now. I just wanna get some sleep."

***

Keith came home and went straight to baby Zakiea's basinet. He barely spoke to Natalie as he walked through the door and into their bedroom. Natalie had to remind him to take off his gun before picking up the baby. But his demeanor was much like a zombie. He was drunk and his eyes were glazed over. For the past three hours he had been at Johnny's, alone, drinking Wild Turkey right out the bottle until the bartender refused to serve him anymore. Stanton's words continued to swirl around in his head all day long. Unable to concentrate at work, he just went through the motions and let

Jason take the lead all day. Now that's he's home, his only desire at the moment was to hold his new baby daughter. He just picked her up and held her tight in his arms making sure to cup her head. Gazing upon her eyes for what seemed like an eternity, the thought of him being fired and disgraced, or even worse in jail, haunted him. Natalie didn't say anything at first. She gave him a little space, but as she noticed that Keith was drunk and his behavior was strange, she knew something was wrong.

"Keith what's wrong baby," she asked with a look of concern on her face.

"Nothing! What's wrong with a man holding his baby?" Keith replied raising his voice. The bass in his voice woke up the baby as she started to cry loudly.

"Something is wrong when you coming home late, drunk, and acting funny." She walked over and took the baby out of his arms. Grabbing the pacifier, she placed it in the babies' mouth quickly and began to rock her back to sleep.

Keith didn't respond. He left the room with his head down and went into the kitchen. Sitting in a chair across from the refrigerator he noticed the magnets holding up the recent pictures of his family leaving the hospital. With his head in his hands, he sat there staring at them. After Natalie calmed the baby down and put her back to sleep, she came storming into the kitchen.

"What the hell is going on with you?"

Natalie's head was tilted to the side and her round eyes were blinking profusely.

Keith took a deep breath, "Natalie, you know I love you and the children right?" He grabbed Natalie by the wrist and pulled her down to where she sat next to him at the kitchen table.

"Of course!" She touched him softly on the face. "Why don't you tell me what's bothering you?"

"I wish I could."

"C'mon, you know you can tell me anything baby."

"I know, but not this time. Not until I get grasp on this situation at work. Until then, it's best you don't know too much."

"What are you talking about? You're not making any sense."

"Well, you've asked me about how I got the extra money lately."

"Yeah! So this has something to do with that?"

"In a round about sort of way. Look, I can't get into anymore details. The less you know the better. But know this. I will do the right thing for you and this family," he explained leaning forward and giving Natalie a hug.

CHAPTER 15

The phone rang at the Love house about six in the morning. It woke Ren out of a sound deep sleep. His first reaction was to look at the alarm clock, but he couldn't get his eyes to focus right away. He reached for the phone on the dresser and answered.

"Yeah," he said sitting up wiping the matter out his eyes.

"Ren, this is Manny. I'm at the Eastside Motel on Bruton. We got a major problem."

"What is it?"

"A South Sider is dead."

"Ah shit! I'm on my way."

Ren hung up the phone and rolled out of bed. He quickly got dressed and went to Michael's room to wake him up. "Hey buddy."

"Daddy," Michael answered peeling of the covers and sitting up on the pillow.

"I got to go to work early so I can't take you to school, Momma is."

"It's okay daddy. I understand."

"Good. I'll try to get home early and we'll

go outside and practice working on your swing. Okay?"

"Okay." Ren leaned over and kissed Michael on the forehead. He tucked him back in and Michael falls back to sleep instantly.

***

Ren pulled up to the Eastside Motel thirty minutes after he got the call. This motel was as rundown as they come. The buildings exterior looked like it had been painted over several times with no primer, cracked and peeling. Beer bottles and crack vials decorated the flower beds instead of beautiful plants. The odor was strong and foul. It smelled like a couple dozen bums surrounded the building and urinated on the walls in unison. Roaches would be a common site in your room. They had gotten so bold, to where they wouldn't even run when the lights got turned on. These were the kind of rooms you could pay for by the hour, if you know what I'm saying.

Manny and Dwayne were already there, but Jason and Keith hadn't arrived yet. Ren walked through the uniform cops at the scene and into the room where the murder took place. The victims were already in body bags, and CSU was gathering evidence, taking pictures, and getting finger prints.

"Ren glad you're here." Manny walked up and greeted him.

"What do we have?" Ren said sipping on a cup of coffee he got from one of the uniform cops on duty.

"We got two victims with multiple gun shot wounds to the head. One is some woman we haven't been able to identify as of yet. The other is Juan Guerra; he's the cousin of Torch," Manny said running his fingers through his well oiled hair.

"Torch's cousin. Ah shit! Who would do something this damn stupid?"

"Look over here." Manny pointed to the wall behind Ren. On it was PG's written in black spray paint.

"What the hell were they thinking? This can start a war for sure," Ren said shaking his head.

"I know."

Ren walked over to the gurney as they were ready to wheel off the victims. Unzipping the body bag, he took a long look at Juan. Juan had two bullet hole wounds right in the chest. He grimaced as he closed it back. Then he stepped over to the other bag, unzipped it, and gasped at what he saw. It was Samantha. She had been shot in the ear and in the mouth. He closed up the body-bag and bowed his head.

"That motherfucker!"

"What?" Manny said with an inquisitive look on his face.

"This wasn't about Juan or the South Siders. This was about revenge for Momo and the heat we're putting on his business."

"I don't follow you."

"The woman in the body bag, her name is Samantha Richards. She is a C.I of mines. She came to me the other day and told me that Red was planning something, but I never suspected it was something like this."

"How can you be so sure? I mean Red already knew he would have to fall in line with us or lose his protection," Manny whispered.

"This motel is where she commonly turns tricks. And take a look at the powder burns on her ear. She was shot from point blank range execution-style. They only killed Juan 'cause he was in the room."

"So, Juan just happened to be the poor bastard getting a blow job at the wrong time. Hmm, so what the hell are we going to do now?"

"Okay, Manny I want you to use your connections and get a twenty on Red's location. Chances are he's posted up at that barbershop," then Ren turned to Dwayne. "I want you to run-down Red's number two, Tony B."

"What you gonna do?" Dwayne asked pulling out his can of Copenhagen to dip some more snuff.

"I'm gonna go have a conversation with Torch. Better he hears the news about Juan's death from me."

The CSU team had finished collecting their evidence and was packing up their equipment to leave. The bodies had been wheeled out and placed in the Coroner's van. Walking through the door as everything was wrapping up was Jason. He took in the crime scene as he made his way to the rest of the guys.

"What's up fellas?"

"You're late," Ren snapped feeling irritated from the whole situation.

"Sorry, there was a lot of traffic."

"You can go with Manny. He'll bring you up to speed," Ren said as he turned and headed for the door.

"Hold on a second Ren. Can I get a word with you?"

"Yeah."

Jason caught up to him as Ren was walking towards his car. "Ren I think we have a problem with Keith. You know when Stanton came into the clubhouse asking to speak with Keith the other day. Well, I got a little suspicious and I walked in on their conversation. It looked liked your boy Keith was rattled, like he was going to break or something. I don't think Stanton was in there to tie up loose ends. I think he's fishing for something," Jason said with his arms folded.

"Stanton has got an axe to grind, and I know what it is."

"What?"

"Remember the chick I picked up at Johnny's the other night. You know the one I won the bet with?"

"Yeah, what about her?"

"Well, I just found out that she's Stanton's wife."

"Goddamn Ren! You sure know how to pick'em."

"I know, and my gut is telling me that he knows about me and Heather. If I'm right he's going to do everything he can to bring down, not only me, but the whole Ghost Squad."

"Okay, so what's the next move?"

"I've been thinking about it, and you're right. Stanton has something on Keith that he's using for leverage. We need to find out what it is."

"How?"

Ren was silent for a minute. He paced back and forth rubbing his chin. "I got it!" he said finally breaking the silence. "Heather says that he works at home. That's our way in," he said snapping his fingers.

"I don't follow?"

"I'll explain it to you later. Get going with Manny. Oh, call Child Protective Services and have them send someone to Woodland City Apartments door number 9034. There are two young boys there that just became orphans."

"Got it. You want me to tell Dwayne and Manny about Keith."

"No! No need to create panic. We'll keep this between us for right now. Not a word to anyone, including Keith. Matter of fact, I'm taking him outta play. I'll give him some paperwork to do for the time being."

"Understood," Jason said reluctantly.

***

Raceway Paint and Body Shop was the unofficial headquarters of the South Siders gang. It was an older grayish looking building that was on a corner lot. Very little body work is done there anymore. The place, when it's not being used for a meeting area, is used to chop up stolen cars. They could take a brand new Lincoln Navigator and totally strip it down and have the parts ready to ship out in under an hour. Ren pulled up and parked right in front of the building. He walked up and asked one of the soldiers to see Torch. The soldier nods and heads into one of the garages to get him.

The South Siders are a very ruthless and violent street gang. They have grown in numbers and have become the most powerful gang of any ethnic background in the Pleasant Grove area. Drugs are their main source of business and a year ago, thanks to Ren and the Ghost Squad, they agreed to divide the neighborhood into two sections. One is controlled by them the other by the PG's. The South Siders are made up exclusively of Mexicans that come from across the border. Most people in Texas commonly refer to these people as "Wet Backs".

The leader was a man name Fernando Venezuela, otherwise known as Torch. He got the nickname because he worked as a welder in the body shop since he was fourteen. He is dark skinned and tall for the average Mexican about six-foot tall. His face looked like it was made of stone, rugged and without emotion. On his face he bore the black tattooed tear drop under his right eye for the five year stretch he did for drug possession. In excellent shape, his body resembles the prison build from his days inside. Walking out the back wearing a white tank-top and pair of heavily starched Dickies, he gestures to one of his subordinates to allow Ren to step forward.

"What's up homez?" Torch said in that thick Mexican accent of his.

"Torch I need to get a word with you."

Torch just stared at Ren for a second wearing a nasty look on his face. Reaching into his pocket he pulled out a box of Kool Filter Kings. Grabbing a cigarette out of the box, he lit it, and after a long drag he exhaled and stepped closer to Ren. "You come here to tell me that my cousin is dead. 'Cause if that's what you're here for, you're too late. Word is already out."

"Okay Torch I know you're mad, but let me get a word with you."

"It's too late for talking homez. The PG's want a war, cool. We're ready to go to the mattresses."

"Can you just hear me out? Give me five minutes," Ren pleaded standing tall and unwavering, but still managing to have a hint of sympathy in his voice.

Torch looked at one of his soldiers, then looked back at Ren and gestured for Ren to follow him inside the garage. They walked to a secluded corner out of the hearing range of any South Side soldier.

"I'm listening," Torch said dropping his cigarette butt to the ground.

"It wasn't a hit on Juan. They were after the girl that was in the motel room with him."

"Bullshit!"

"It's true. She was a C.I of mines. Red had her killed to get back at me for poppin Momo's ass."

"I don't give a shit if she was your wife. Someone is going to pay for killing a South Sider, ese."

"What if I could deliver Red to you?"

"You fuckin' with me?"

"No, I'm serious. What if I deliver Red to your door step? Give you your revenge. Would you continue to honor your deal with the PG's and keep the peace?"

"You deliver that mayate to me and we'll stay cool Ese. You got twenty four hours. But if he's not here by then, bodies are gonna start dropping. Comprende?"

"Twenty-four hours. He'll be here."

***

Keith had awoken late this morning with a terrible hangover. He turned and looked at his alarm clock that was still going off. Fumbling around for a second, he finally managed to get his coordination together long enough to hit the off button. He reached to his side to feel for Natalie, but she wasn't there. *She's probably feeding the baby* he thought. His head was pounding like someone was hitting him upside the head with sledgehammer. Staggering to his feet, he walked over to the dresser where his phone was at. Opening it up, he saw that he'd missed dozens of calls. Some from the night before, but most seemed to be from this morning. He scrolled threw the names until he got to Ren's and he pushed send.

"Yeah," Ren answered.

"I'm sorry I'm just returning your call. I'm not feeling too good."

"What's wrong?"

"Allergies," Keith answered. It was the first quick lie that came to Keith's mind. Ren knew that Keith struggled from time to time with nasal allergies, so he was likely to believe that.

"That's all, nothing else bothering you? Jason thought you were acting a little strange yesterday," Ren said trying to casually probe giving Keith the opportunity to maybe reveal something that happen.

"Ah, no, I mean you know how those anti-histamines can make your head foggy."

"Yeah I know. So are you coming in today or what?"

"Yeah, what you got me doing?"

"Go to the office and finish up the paperwork

on the Harris case and get it over to Division."

"Okay."

"Alright, hope you feel better. Later," Ren said hanging up the phone.

Keith got dressed and walked in the living room to see Natalie with the baby on the couch. She was breastfeeding Zekia who was starting to get a little bit restless. She had been lying in the playpen all morning while Natalie straightened up the house, cooked breakfast, and got Jacob off to school.

"How are you feeling this morning?" Natalie asked flipping through the channels with the remote control, while holding the baby in the other hand.

"I'll live," Keith murmured making his way into the kitchen to get a cup of coffee. He grabbed a slice of toast off the serving platter on the counter and started heading for the front door.

"You should really sit down and get some food in you. You'll feel better."

"No time. I'm already late." He kissed her on the cheek before opening the front door. The blazing heat and glare from the uncovered sun hit Keith in the face abruptly, causing him to see blackness for a second.

"Keith, I know this ain't a good time, but are we going to talk about what happened last night?"

"We'll talk when I get home. See you tonight."

Keith arrived at The Ship around noon. The lobby was already full with suspects, people filing complaints, and officers doing their normal paperwork. The customary sound of fingers hitting keyboards and the shuffling of papers filled the air like always. He walked through trying to be as inconspicuous as possible. Avoiding Stanton was his number one goal. He knew the moment Stanton saw him he would want to continue the conversation that was interrupted by Jason yesterday, and that's the last thing he wants to deal with until he could get his thoughts together. All Keith needed was to get into the clubhouse without being seen by him. He could finish the paperwork Ren had him doing without ever having to leave the room. All the files he needed were already in there.

Keith managed to creep by the Watch Commander without being noticed. He saw that the Captain's office door was closed, so he slid by it. He stopped just before getting to the breakroom. The breakroom served as a mini cafeteria. It had a couple of tables, a refrigerator, microwave, and vending machines. It was separated from the lobby by glass walls. He peeped around the corner and saw that nobody was in there, and he briskly walked the short distance to the clubhouse. He backed in the office slowly closing the door doing one last check to make sure that Stanton was nowhere in sight.

"Hello."

Keith closed the door quickly and turned around. It was Stanton sitting down in one of the chairs with his feet propped up on the table. He was picking his teeth with a toothpick.

"What the hell are you doing in here?" Keith said walking over and leaning against the table. "Only the Ghost Squad is allowed in here!"

"Waiting on you. We got unfinished business."

"You shouldn't be here!"

"Don't worry. I over heard that the Ghost Squad caught a gang related murder this morning."

"So you're spying on us now?"

"Should I be?"

Keith glanced at Stanton with a look of frustration on his face. He didn't say anything, he just rubbed his mustache.

"Should I be?" Stanton repeated the question.

"Just leave me the hell alone!" Keith said turning and walking back to the door.

"This just ain't going to go away Sanders."

Keith stopped at the door with his back facing Stanton. Stanton stood up and took a step forward.

"You know what I'm holding in my hands? It's an affidavit from Wendell Pierce, the attorney of record for one Morris Jones. He states that he personally witness Mr. Jones placing approximately five hundred thousand dollars in his wall safe the day before he was killed. The same safe that you just happened to leave your fingerprints on and now that safe is empty and there's no trace of the money. You see the money was part of the proceeds of a legitimate business deal that Mr. Pierce had brokered for him," Stanton said handing Keith a copy of the affidavit.

Keith looked over the papers and was astonished at what he saw.

"You know what I think happened that morning? I think a group of cops used a situation to their advantage and extorted money from a drug dealer. I don't believe Momo ever had a chance to leave that house alive. It's only a matter of time before all the pieces fall into place," Stanton said coldly.

Keith suddenly became paralyzed with fear. Stanton reached for another file he had in his briefcase.

"You know what else I got here? I'm holding your financials. You have quite the lifestyle Mr. Sanders. A hundred and fifty thousand dollar mortgage and two car loans on a cops pay seems a little excessive. Especially for a man whose wife doesn't work," Stanton revealed. "I wonder what else I'll find if I keep digging? What other connections you and the Ghost Squad have to Momo? You think your boys will hold up under the pressure when it's their ass in a sling. You think they'll keep their mouth shut and go down when jail time starts being involved. Someone will give it up, they always do. And when that happens, you'll be the one behind bars while those guys are out living their lives. We're talking about a possible murder charge here. You know what that means? That means if you go down, by the time you get out, that little girl of yours will be graduating from high school."

Keith had a single tear starting to roll down his cheek. He could envision the entire scenario that Stanton had laid out for him, and the thought of not being there for his children was something that shook him to his very soul. The struggle within was ripping him apart. His convictions had been tested on both sides. On one hand, loyalty and friendship to the Ghost Squad were things that he held sacred, especially his friendship with Ren. Ren had been his best friend for more than thirty years. He felt obligated to him, but on the other hand, he had a family that he was responsible for. Natalie and the kids are his heart, and the guilt that he was living with became too much of a weight to bear. Going to the confessional at St. Mary's and asking for absolution brought him no solace. He turned around slowly and spoke with a soft cracking voice, "I'll tell you what I know, but I want immunity from any charges."

"You tell me your side and if it checks out I'll get you immunity."

"No! You give me immunity first or no fucking deal."

Stanton hesitated for a minute. He looked

Keith up and down, "Okay. You have immunity, but I can't guarantee anything as far as
your job goes."

"I don't give a shit," Keith replied.

"Alright, so what happened?"

"I want it in writing, signed by the D.A before I tell you anything."

"That'll take time."

"Well, get back to me when it's done."

CHAPTER 16

McCain and Bernstein were back at The Ship after another grueling eighteen-hour day. They were on their way to meet with Captain Riley. The Captain was starting to really feel the pressure from police headquarters. With the *Hands off Killer* being credited with a third murder, the public was starting to demand answers. Every type of women's group you can imagine from the Urban League to the Ladies of Distinction were calling the Mayor's office and expressing their concerns. An emergency meeting at City Hall was scheduled to address the situation and try to ease the tension. Even restaurant and club owners were concern because business was down. Women of all kind were terrified to go out at night.

Captain Riley and the Deputy Police Chief were sitting in the Captain's office when McCain and Bernstein walked in.

"Gentlemen have a seat," said the Captain.

The laid back atmosphere that usually exists

in the Captain's office felt much more uptight. They sat down in front of the Captain who was behind his desk, and the Deputy Police Chief standing to his right in full dress uniform holding his hat. The stars on his shoulder and medals on his chest sparkled under the lights in the office. His patent leather shoes were perfectly polished, and his posture along with his intense stare showed that he was strictly business.

"Guys, I think you've both met Deputy Chief Brown before?"

"Yes sir," they both answered as they reached over and shook his hand firmly.

"I was just letting the Captain here know that The Ship has been given carte blanche to do whatever is necessary to close this case. I'm here to give you guys any type of support you need, surveillance teams, overtime, what ever you need. The Mayor and the Chief want to make sure you have all resources at your disposal," Chief Brown said sitting at the edge of the Captain's desk.

"Thank you sir," they both responded.

Chief Brown stood up, put on his hat, and turned toward the Captain. "Update me as soon as you know anything."

"Yes sir." Chief Brown exited the office and all three men breathed a sigh of relief.

"He's been on my ass all morning. I've been getting calls from the mayor's office every hour on the hour wanting new updates on the case. I hope you two have turned up something," the

Captain said leaning back in his chair grimacing.

"Well, our canvas of Cynthia Morrow's crime scene turned up next to nothing. Only thing we got were some fingerprints from inside the house. No witnesses to the murder. Forensics has turned up nothing. Her family said that she hasn't been seeing anyone as of late. None of the neighbors or family recognized our mystery man on the sketch or the vehicle. We got nothing," McCain admitted.

"So the only thing about this victim that's related to the other two victims is that they were killed in the same fashion," the Captain pointed out. "Maybe it's about time we start exploring other angles? Isn't it's possible that there could be another connection you're over looking?"

McCain shook his head, "I don't think so. The M.E said that the murders were committed by the same person, and I don't think it's a coincidence that our mystery man has been connected to all of them."

"There's obviously a connection, but what's the motive. These murders don't appear to be crimes-of-passion to me. It's possible there's something else linking these murders. Look, I know you McCain. Once you focus in on something you get tunnel vision. I'm only asking that you just keep an open mind, alright? A lot of people are watching on this. I'm going to give you a little latitude, but I expect results."

"I understand."

"By the way, I had Cynthia Morrow's phone records pulled. It maybe nothing, but it seems she had a call from a throwaway cell phone two months ago. We traced the sell of the phone to a store in Balch Springs. You guys should get out there and check it out. Who knows, it might be a lead."

***

Business was slow at the Super One Food Mart when McCain and Bernstein pulled into the parking lot around noon. The temperature was around ninety degrees and the air conditioner was turned up to the max in the unmarked Ford Taurus they were riding in. Both men loosened their ties and took off their suit coats while getting out the car.

"Maybe the Captain is right McCain. It could be another connection."

"Bernstein how long you've been a cop?" McCain inquired as he stopped walking and turned towards Bernstein to look him in the eye.

"Ten years."

"And of those ten years, how many years you spent working homicide?"

"Four, but what's that got to do with anything?"

"Plenty! What the hell do you know about investigating? You're not a true cop; you're an opportunist looking for another way to climb up the ladder. That's the only reason you're here, to further your career," McCain ranted.

"Oh, and you don't have your own personal reasons for wanting to be on this case. I looked in your file McCain. Two bad marriages, one of which your wife cheated on you. And now you want to throw all the police resources into bringing the cheating husband into custody. Who's the opportunist now?"

"My marriages failed because I put my job first. Can you say the same?"

Bernstein was quiet as he looked away for a second.

"I thought so. Now you might have the lieutenant bars, but I'm in charge of this case. So, if I feel that the cheating husband who's been dating women on the side did it, that's the angle we're going to pursue!" McCain said forcefully as he began to walk towards the store.

They walked in to see the owner behind the counter reading the morning newspaper. He was a Middle Eastern man who was heavy set with a five o'clock shadow and a thick mustache. The first thing McCain noticed as he walked through the door was the surveillance camera pointed at him as he headed for the front counter.

"Excuse me sir, we need to ask you a few questions," McCain said as he and Bernstein pulled out their badges and flashed them to the owner.

"Hello my friends. My licenses are current. I always check the ID before selling the alcohol. And I ..." The owner tried explaining in a thick

Middle-Eastern accent.

"We're not here for that sir," McCain interrupted. "There was a cell phone that was sold a couple of months back. Do you think you can remember who you sold it to?" McCain asked handing him a sheet of paper with the information of the time and date on it.

The owner looked down at the date, "This was two months ago! I sell lots of cell phones."

"Why don't you check your receipts, maybe he paid with a credit card?"

"Okay, just a minute."

He went into his office and opened up a huge filing cabinet. He looked through the rolls of register tape until he got to the month of March. He skimmed through the day's sales in question, and found the one they were looking for.

"I sold one phone that day and they paid cash."

"Damn!" McCain blurted out. "What about your surveillance tapes for that day?"

"I tape over them every other day."

McCain stood there grinding his teeth. Then he reached into his pocket and pulled out a folded up copy of the sketch they'd been circulating. "Have you ever seen this man?"

"Yes. He comes in every now and then. He very nice guy. He buy phone from here before. He do something wrong?"

McCain looked at Bernstein with a sarcastic grin then turned his attention back to the store owner. "Well, we need to get a hold of him so that we can ask him some questions. Do you know his name?"

"Sorry, but I don't know his name?"

"Okay, well if you see him again please give us a call," McCain said reaching into the lapel of his suit coat and handing the owner his business card. "Thanks for your help."

"No problem."

They began to walk back to the car when McCain's cell phone rang.

"Hello."

"McCain this is Captain Riley, we got a hit on that fingerprint from Cynthia Morrow's home. It belongs to Andre Mason. He has a prior record for domestic violence. This might be our guy."

"Great! What's the address?"

"8500 West Ave."

"Okay we're en route. Have units meet us there."

"I'm on it."

McCain hung the phone and turned to Bernstein, "We gotta hit on that fingerprint. Let's go. I'll drive; you call Judge Moore and get us a search warrant for his home."

***

They pulled up at the corner house at the end of the block. Other police units arrived at the same time. Everyone hopped out their cars, in McCain's case slowly crept out because of his bad knees, and huddled together. McCain walked to the back of his car and pulled out a little heavier artillery, a twelve gauge shot gun to be exact. While grabbing that, he also pulled out two bulletproof vests and handed one to Bernstein. Another police car approached shortly after. It was Captain Riley himself making a rare appearance at the site of an arrest.

"Here's the search warrant," the Captain proclaim as he handed it to McCain.

"Thank you Captain. You didn't have to come."

"Oh yes I did. The chief wants an update immediately!"

"I understand," McCain said taking the warrant from the Captain and turning his attention back towards the uniform cops who were waiting.

"Okay everyone listen up. I want cars covering the street and alley at both ends to cut off escape routes," McCain motioned with his hands. "You two take the rear exit; me and Bernstein will hit the front door. And remember, we're dealing with a possible serial killer here, so be prepared for anything."

Everyone nodded their heads and assumed their positions. McCain and Bernstein walked up the porch to the front door. They looked through the curtains to see if they could see anyone, then they knocked on the door. They heard the click of the lock and the door squeaked open. An elderly woman opened the door.

"Hello," she said with a smile.

"Afternoon Miss. We're detectives with the Dallas Police Deparment. Is there an Andre Mason living here?" Bernstein asked politely as both he and McCain slid their handguns to their sides so that the women couldn't see them.

"Yes, he's my son. What do you want with him?" The lady replied.

"We just need to ask him a few questions," McCain said.

"Oh, okay," she said as she turned and yelled. "Andre, someone at the door for you!"

"I'm coming momma!" He yelled back.

He walked into the hallway in his boxer shorts and wife-beater. He was scratching his head and walking toward the front door when he spotted the detectives in their bulletproof vests with "Police" written in big letters. His eyes widened and then he took off down the hall.

"Excuse me Miss," Bernstein said as he pushed the door open and took off after him.

Andre quickly headed for the kitchen, but saw that there were uniform cops coming through the back door. Breathing heavily he turned into his room and locked the door behind him just before Bernstein could get to him. Andre swiftly went to the window and opened it up. He climbed out as Bernstein was kicking in the bedroom door. As his bare feet hit the hot concrete, he studied the street for a second to figure out which way to run. He ran to the next door neighbor's house and hopped their fence like he was a world class hurdler.

Bernstein sprinted through the broken down door and pulled out his walkie-talkie radio as he climbed through the window.

"All units be advised, suspect has fled the scene on foot. He went out the east window of the house. He's wearing a white tank-top and blue boxer shorts. The suspect is unarmed. Repeat, suspect is unarmed," Bernstein yelled into the radio as he followed Andre over the fence.

"Stop! Stop!" Bernstein yelled as he followed Andre going over fence after fence, but Andre ignored the order.

Bernstein was starting to gain on him. He was almost close enough to grab him, but Andre was slippery. He twisted his body and changed direction so that Bernstein couldn't get a grip on him. Andre went over the last fence at the end of the block, but was stun by what he saw when he cleared the last fence. A sea of cops with their guns drawn and yelling in unison, "Freeze!"

He stopped then was hit hard from the back. It was Bernstein who had a knee in his back. He slapped the cuffs on Andre in seconds. So pissed that he had to rundown Andre, Bernstein used Andre's head as a prop so he could stand back up. McCain finally caught up, as he was in a slow trot. He holstered his weapon and helped

Bernstein bring Andre to his feet.

"Nice work," McCain said with a smirk.

Andre's mother fought through the cluster of police that was surrounding her son. She was still wearing a long night gown, house shoes, and a head scarf. "What are y'all doing to my son?" Andre's mother asked elbowing her way through the sea of cops.

"Your son is a suspect in a murder investigation, Miss," McCain replied dryly, as they began to lead him away and into the back of a squad car.

"Murder!" Andre yelled, "I ain't murdered no one. There's got to be some kind of mistake!"

"Andre Mason you got the right to remain silent, if you give up the right to remain silent, anything you say can and will be held against you in a court of law. You have the right to and attorney, if you cannot afford an attorney one we'll be provided to you," Berstein said as he shoved Andre into the backseat by the head.

***

They arrived at The Ship, and immediately led Andre to an interrogation room. The interrogation rooms at The Ship looked like dungeon, cold and uninviting. It had four concrete walls; one of them was equipped with a one-way mirror. The only thing in this room was two chairs and a metal table with a hook on it to cuff someone's hands to. McCain, the Captain, Bernstein, and a team of detectives walked into the adjoining room and were preparing to discuss a plan of attack on how to question Andre Mason while looking at him through the window. McCain took charge as he normally does in situations like this and started giving people assignments.

"Evans, come here," McCain said to the uniform duty officer that was standing in the doorway.

"Yes sir," he replied.

"I want you to turn up the heat in the interrogation room to ninety-degrees. Then I want you to offer our friend in there something to drink about every five minutes. Got it?" McCain said looking at his watch.

"Yes sir," he said leaving the room quickly to execute his orders.

"Stevenson, I need you to pull all the phone records for the last six months and cross reference them against the other two victims. See if he's had any contact with them. Barber, I want you to contact Mrs. Gordon and get a lineup ready. And Davis, I need you to run a search through DMV, see if Mason, his mother, or any of his friends have a blue Ford Mustang registered to their names."

The detectives all nodded and went off to perform their tasks as McCain picked up Andre's file and began to scan over his criminal history.

"So what are we going to do here? You want me to go in first and soften him up or what?" Bernstein inquired.

"No. We're gonna wait first. You got to be patient. You know there's an old saying. You can take frog and drop him in hot water and he'll jump right out. But if you put him in cold water and turn up the heat, he'll cook to death. That's what we're doing with Andre, literally, we're going to turn up the heat and watch him sweat," McCain said while the Captain let out a slight grunt.

They stood at the one-way mirror watching Andre sweat up a storm, and gulp down sodas, one after another. He got more and more nervous with every passing second. Standing up every few minutes, he would rub his hands together and pace back and forth. Finally, after about thirty minutes passed by, McCain went in.

"Mr. Mason, it seems we got a lot to talk about," McCain stated taking a seat across from Andre and placing the file folder on the table.

"You must be the detective in charge. Sir, there's gotta be some kind of mistake. I didn't murder anyone. I only ran because I thought you came to arrest me for a warrant on some tickets I didn't pay," Andre explained popping his knuckles and breathing hard.

"Calm down. First of all, why don't you tell me where you were between midnight and two in the morning yesterday?"

"I was.... I was at home watching TV last

night," Andre stuttered, "Why?"

"Because Cynthia Morrow was murdered last night."

"Oh my God!" Andre cried out closing his eyes and bowing his head on the table. He took a deep breath and looked back up, "You don't... you don't think I had something to do with her death?"

"Your fingerprints are in her bedroom."

"Well, yeah, I mean we were...you know, lovers?" Andre stammered out.

"So how long had you been seeing her?"

"We met a couple of months back at Club Blue. We went out a few times, but it was nothing serious," Andre answered as he took another swallow of the fourth soda he was working on. "Say, why is it so hot in here?" Andre asked pulling on the front of his shirt trying to use it like a fan.

"I'm sorry about that. Air conditioning is out. Maintenance is working on it right now. They should have it fixed shortly," McCain lied.

"Can I go to the bathroom? I really need to take a piss," Andre asked as he began to squirm around in his seat. The drinks had begun to take their toll. His bladder was starting to feel the pressure.

"In a minute, I want to finish getting your statement first. Now, back to Cynthia Morrow, when was the last time you saw her?"

"I haven't seen her in over a week. Like I

said, it was a casual fling," Andre answered.

"A casual fling huh? Cynthia was beautiful, intelligent, and had a good job. Why would she want a casual fling with a man like you?" McCain asked turning up his tone a notch.

"Huh?"

"Well, according to this file I'm looking at, you've been collecting unemployment for the last four months, and you live at home with your mother. I think once she found that out, she cut you loose."

"No, it's not like that at all."

"Sure it is. Why would any woman want dead weight like you? Isn't that why you killed her? Because when she found out that you're just some freeloading Momma's boy, she knew she could do better?" McCain said emphatically as he stood up and got in Andre's face.

Andre continued to constantly readjust himself in his seat. The pressure on that bladder of his was continuing to mount. The heat in the interrogation room was sweltering. McCain had no intentions at all of turning on the air conditioner, or letting him go to the bathroom until he gave a full confession. Andre wiped away the sweat from his forehead trying to keep his composure under the stress of the situation. "That's not true. That's not true! She cared about me," Andre said.

"Cared about you, she didn't give a rat's ass about you. She couldn't wait to be finished with you. She was trying to spare your pathetic feelings. Isn't that right?"

"No, she cared about me. She liked me. She just had a hard time committing. She wasn't ready to settle down yet."

"So that's the reason why you killed her, because she didn't want to commit to you? Is that why you cut off her hands, you sick son-of-bitch, so you could guarantee she wouldn't touch anyone else!" McCain barked as he slammed his hands down on the table.

"No, no, I didn't kill her," Andre whimpered as he pissed his pants.

McCain looked deep into Andre's eyes as he quivered in fear. McCain, who had done hundreds of interrogations during his career, had become a master of reading people. Then the door opened, and a tall white lady wearing a pantsuit and carrying a briefcase walked through. "I'm Shelia Edmonds; I've been hired by Mrs. Mason as counsel. What the hell is going on here detective?" She asked putting her briefcase on the table and giving McCain a dirty look, "This interview is over. I need to speak with my client in private."

McCain walked out to see the Captain standing in the hallway.

"We tried to hold her off as long as possible," the Captain said. "So what do you think?"

"I could have used a few more minutes," McCain replied.

Detective Barber walked up with Bernstein. "Ms. Gordon is here McCain, we're ready for the lineup," Barber said.

"Here goes the file the detectives were able to work up so far," Bernstein reported as he handed the files to McCain.

McCain started scanning over the information. "There's no connection at all to the other women. His cell phone is not the one sold at the store, his mother's phone shows no calls to any of the women, and nobody he knows has access to a Mustang," he remarked.

The door to the interrogation room reopened and Shelia stepped out. "I don't approve of your tactics here Captain. I will file a complaint," she snapped.

"Complain all you want. Your client was properly Mirandize. We got four murders in which your client is a suspect," the Captain responded.

"Are you charging my client with murder?" She snapped.

"We're holding Mr. Mason pending a lineup first," McCain added.

They all walked into another observation room. It also had a one-way mirror that looked upon the lineup room. It's just like what you would see in the movies. There's a small stage were five guys walk on to, and lines running along the back wall to show you the men's height. Bernstein escorted Ms. Gordon in as she shivered a bit from the cold temperatures in the room. The door opened on the other side and the men walked in single file and turned around

THE HANDS OF LOVE · 189

to face the mirror.

"All right Ms. Gordon, you can see them but they can't see you. You're completely safe in here," McCain stated calmly. "Just look over the men and tell me if you see the one that was with your daughter."

"Okay," she answered as she put on her glasses and studied the men closely.

McCain hit the intercom button and instructed all the men to turn left, then back forward again. "Take your time and let us know if you see him."

"Or if you don't see him," Shelia interjected.

"Quiet counselor," the Captain snapped, "You're here only as a courtesy."

"I don't see him," Ms. Gordon said.

"Are you sure?" McCain asked.

"I remember that face anywhere. These guys sort of look like him, but he's not here."

"Thank you Ms. Gordon. You've been a big help. If we need you again we'll be in contact," McCain said as Bernstein escorted her out.

"So I'm guessing my client is free to go?" Shelia proclaimed.

"Yeah, he's free to go," McCain responded reluctantly.

Shelia left the room immediately. The Captain closed the door as she left and stepped closer to McCain, "Are you sure you know what you're doing? He's been our only lead so far."

"He didn't do it Captain," McCain answered

as he paused for a second. "Andre Mason is a naïve kid, not a criminal mastermind able to conceal evidence and cover his tracks. He pissed on himself in interrogation, hardly the type of behavior of a stone cold killer of three women. No, our guy is still out there."

CHAPTER 17

Ren was sitting at a table in the food court at Towneast Mall. It was around three in the afternoon. The mall was moderately being shopped. He had just finished polishing off a sub sandwich and was eagerly awaiting his secret meeting. That's why he chose the mall. Ren was looking at his watch and back at the escalators observing the people coming and going. Then he saw him. Brian Peterson came walking up fast with an irritated look on his face. Brian was a former investment banker that Ren got out of a jam a few years back. He is a small fragile white man with a receding hairline. He saw Ren, walked over, and took a seat across from him.

"What the hell am I doing here Ren? I thought we were finished," Brian snapped.

"Not yet, I got one more thing I need you to do."

Brian shook his head, "This is not fair. I've done enough Ren."

"I saved your ass Brian, got you out of a jam

with the Justice Department. I gave you a fresh start. If it wasn't for me, you'd be grabbing your ankles for the brothers up in Leavenworth. I think I deserve one last favor," Ren said sitting up straight."

"What is it?"

"You still got your contacts in the Cayman Islands right?"

"Yeah."

"I got some cash that needs to be washed," Ren whispered.

"So you want me to do the very thing I nearly got busted for. You must think I'm an idiot?" Brian said as his face got flushed and he nervously looked side to side.

"It's not like that at all. This is personal, a one time thing. You see I got a friend of mines that's got some cash. He needs to make a legitimate big purchase, but he can't use it without bringing unnecessary attention to himself."

"How soon do you need this done?"

"By Sunday."

"That's really pushing it."

"I know, but this will be the last favor I ask you. You got my word on that."

"All right," Brian said rubbing the knees of his pants.

"Now how will this work?"

"You give me the cash and my guy cuts you a check from one of his finance companies for a loan. It's technically a loan, but obviously you never have to repay it and it raises no red flags.

He takes eight cents on the dollar for the standard fee."

"Good."

"So who's name will I have him make the check out for and how much cash we're talking about," Brian asked pulling out a small piece of paper and a pen.

"A hundred and twenty thousand, and use the name Cedric Douglas."

"When will you have the money?"

"As soon as I see the check with that name on it."

"Okay, I'll be in touch."

"And lighten up some. You need to learn how to relax," Ren joked lightly tapping Brian on the shoulder.

Brian looked at Ren without acknowledging his comment. Agitated, Brian stood up and quickly took off toward the mall exit without so much as a goodbye. Ren started making his way to the parking lot right at the food court entrance. He didn't have to walk far because he parked in the police marked spot right next to the handicap parking. He got outside when his phone rang,

"Yeah."

"Ren this is Manny. I got a twenty on Tony B."

"Good, where you at?" Ren asked.

"We're headed east on Military Pkwy. We just crossed over Dolphin Rd," Manny replied.

"Okay, sit tight and hold your position; I'm

coming your way," Ren said hanging up the phone and then dialing Dwayne. "Dwayne, got anything on Red yet?"

"No. I tried everywhere, the barbershop, his' place, girlfriend's crib, nobody's seen his ass," Dwayne reported.

"Okay, it's obvious that word has spread that he hit a South Sider. He's gonna lay low, so we'll have to use Tony B to find him. I need you to get back to The Ship and requisition us a cargo van. Hit me back when you're done."

"Got it," Dwayne said hanging up.

***

Ren caught up to Manny and Jason who were parked across the street and a half block down from the small rundown house that Tony B went into. Now Tony B and Ren had major history together. You see not only were Ren and Keith good friends growing up, but he was also good friends with Tony B at one point in time. All three would routinely hang out back then. From the time they were in grade school all the way up to high school, they were inseparable. You couldn't tell one from the other because they dress so much alike. They all wore tight fitting parachute pants; Adidas with the fat laces, and even went to the same shop so their Jeri Curls would look similar. They even formed a break-dancing group called The Soul Force. Tony B was the first one on the block with a giant jam box. He lugged that thing around on his shoulder like Radio Raheem from *Do the Right Thing*, while Ren and Keith would carry their cardboard mats and challenge other crews to a dance off. Keith was the only guy from the neighborhood that could spin on his head, while Ren's pop-locking skills were second to none.

Things were great until the spring of eighty three, the year before they were to graduate. Tony B loved to shoot craps. He wanted to get in on a game at the gambling shack in South Dallas, but he didn't want to go alone. He begged Ren and Keith to go with him. Keith was totally against it of course, but Ren said he would go. On Saturday they were supposed to meet up, Ren didn't show up. Keith had convinced Ren it was a bad idea to go. Tony B was head strong and wanted to get his gambling on regardless. He went to the spot and got into a game with some hardcore brothers from the south side. Tony B was hitting every lick imaginable, naturals, little joe's, even eight the hard way. He was laughing in the faces of his competitors, who really didn't take kindly to his antics. It was about one in the morning when the game was finally over. Tony B was eight hundred dollars richer. Smiling, Tony B fanned his winnings in the faces of some very soar losers as he was strutting out the door. One of the guys whose money he took was furious. He went to his car and grabbed a twelve gauge shot gun out the trunk. Sneaking up behind the jubilant Tony B, the man took a shot at him but missed when Tony B ducked after someone else yelled gun. Stunned, Tony B stuffed the money he won in his pocket and hauled ass. He sprinted to his car as the guy continued to fire rounds at him. Tony B ran as close as could to the ground while searching for his car keys at the same time. He made it to his car and cranked up the engine quickly. He was so scared that he pulled out too fast and didn't see the pregnant woman that was going into labor and was being helped to her car by her husband. Tony B clipped her when he sped off down the block and killed her and the baby she was carrying instantly. He got out the car and tried to help. The woman's husband was standing over her trying to administer CPR. Tony B waived his hands and yelled for help to anyone that could hear him. One person responded. It was the disgruntled man with the shotgun. He walked right up behind Tony B while he was yelling for help and fired the gauge at his head. The only thing that saved him from getting his head blown clean off, ironically, was the husband who pushed him away as he was trying to provide help. The shot ended up hitting him in the shoulder instead of the head.

At seventeen, Tony B was given five to ten years for involuntary manslaughter. He ended up doing the whole ten years for the inevitable infractions that were necessary for him to make it on the inside. He joined the PG's while in prison, and has been part of the gang ever since. Not to mention, that still to this day, he blames Ren for everything that happened to him. He believed that if Ren had shown up, like he said he would, he would've never gotten shot and consequently, never would've killed that woman.

Ren got out his car and climbed into the backseat of Manny's Maxima. "What's up boys?" Ren said slamming the back door.

"Tony B is driving that white Navigator over there," Manny said pointing to the car sitting down the street. "He went into the brown house on the corner about an hour ago. So why are we following him anyway, Ren?"

"I talked to Torch this morning and he's willing to keep the status-quo, if we deliver Red to him," Ren answered.

"What do you mean deliver Red?" Jason interjected.

"Well, Manny was right. Red is never going to go along with the program. He's never going to get over the whole Momo thing. And now that he's caused a possible war, we got no choice. We have to get rid of him and put someone in place that we can work with. Thanks to Torch, we can knockout two birds with one stone if you will. We deliver Red to Torch and he'll make him disappear, and by default Tony B will take over."

"Why Tony B, the man despises you?" Jason asked.

"We need Tony B to find Red. He's his number two and probably the only person that knows his location. And as far as him hating me, at the end of the day, Tony B is a bottom line guy. His going to do whatever's in his best interest. Believe that!"

"So what's the plan?" Manny asked.

"We can't go in that house without a warrant. Therefore, we're going to wait in the cut until he leaves and pull him over, make it look like a routine traffic stop. It's less confrontational that way. Once we get Red's location, Dwayne is going to meet us there with a cargo van to pick him up," Ren said.

Two hours passed by before Tony B eventually came strolling out the house. Without a doubt he had a rough and rugged exterior. Ten years in a state prison will do that to you. He has what I call a penitentiary build. You know the broad shoulders and chest, large arms, and a small lower body. From his days in prison until now, he works out his upper body far more than the lower. He's sharply dressed in some slacks, an Egyptian cotton shirt, and Dolce and Gabbana shoes. His style is second to none except for one thing. He refuses to let go of his nineteen eighties Jeri Curl that's cut in the shape of a shag. He wore that hairdo before he went to prison, and had it the moment he got out.

As he stepped out the front door, he kissed a young lady on the lips. Pulling the keys out of his pocket, he hit the keypad to turnoff his car alarm. He hopped in his ride and took off down the block.

Manny cranked up his car quickly and followed in close pursuit. Ren decided to park his car and ride with them. Once Tony B got about three or four blocks away, Manny turned on the sirens and had him pullover. Ren got out the backseat and slowly made his way to the driver side window. He tapped on the tinted window, and it came down to reveal a disgusted looking Tony B.

"Ren, I should've known. What the fuck you pull me over for?" Tony B asked angrily.

"Because we need to talk. Step out the vehicle," Ren commanded.

"And what if I don't?"

"Correct me if I'm wrong, but you're a convicted felon. I'm wondering what I'll find if I did a search of this Navigator," Ren said letting his eyes roam across the interior of his car.

Tony B sucked his teeth, cut his eyes at Ren, and reluctantly got out the car. "Make it quick!"

"I got something you need, and you got something I need."

"What's that?"

"Red has stirred up some major shit killing Juan. Whether by accident or not, Torch is ready to go to war over this. But I have a way that we could avoid more blood shed and put everything back to normal. That's where you come in. If we turn Red over to the South Siders they'll let bygones be bygones. With Red out the way you'll be the new king of the PG's."

"Please! I was born at night, not last night. Who do I look like, Sammy Lunchmeat?" Tony B said sarcastically.

"I'm serious," Ren said.

"Nah, fuck that shit. I got too much to lose if shit goes wrong. Besides, I don't trust your ass Ren," Tony B said flashing a mean scowl.

"Look, for once can you get over what happened twenty years ago, it's time you let that shit go."

"Let it go! You were supposed to be there. You were supposed to have my back. 'Cause of you, I got my shoulder blown off. 'Cause of you, I did ten fucking years! Ten years! You have any idea what I went through in prison as a teenager?"

"I'm sorry Tony," Ren said bowing his head. "But forget about our beef for a second and look at the big picture. You got a chance to step up to the big seat. To get what you deserve. What you always wanted. You've been sitting in the wings playing the good soldier for years while young punks like Red run your crew into the ground. At the end of the day, you know that Red will sit in hiding while you guys fight the war for him. Why risk your life and freedom for some asshole's personal vendetta. You owe him nothing."

"All I gotta do is tell you where he's at?" Tony B asked as he turned around and put the palms of his hands on the hood of the car.

"That's it! You'll never hear from Red again."

"How am I going to sell this to my crew?"

"Just tell them that Red got scared and ran like the bitch he is. One more thing, I'm going to need the shooters too."

"Why?"

"I can't have unsolved murders on the books, especially when one of the victims is a civilian. Juan is a soldier he knows the risk, but the girl was innocent. They should've never shot her. Look, there's no murder weapon and I'll make sure that the evidence is flimsy. Your guys plead guilty to two counts of manslaughter and they won't do more than five years tops."

Tony B tapped his nails against the hood of the car in a strange rhythm while mulling over Ren's offer. "Ren if this is some bullshit investigation or anything like that, I'll...."

"You got my word. This is on the up and up," Ren interrupted before Tony B could finish his sentence.

He turned around to face Ren, "Okay".

***

Ren, Jason, and Manny met up with Dwayne at the home of Jamie Summers. She was the little known girlfriend of Red. The Garland area, that's just northeast of Dallas, was the location of her modest home. The three bedroom frame house was located in an older neighborhood. Most of the residents are retirees, or older adults whose children have left the nest. A perfect hideout spot for a youngster like Red who didn't have to worry about running into anybody he knows.

It was nine at night. The sun had just set, and the street lights were beginning to come on. Jamie was in the kitchen frying up Red some catfish for dinner. He was sitting on the couch, relaxing with his shoes off and watching a new episode of, "The Sopranos".

Outside, about three or four houses down, Dwayne was pulling up in a white cargo van behind Manny's parked car. The street was quiet and desolate that night as Dwayne parked the van beside a large tree trying to be inconspicuous. Silently, they quickly got out Manny's car and climbed into the back of the van. They all pulled out their weapons, checked them thoroughly, and loaded them for action. Turning on their walkie-talkies, they all switch them to the same channel. Dressed in all black, the Ghost Squad got out the van and promptly made their way up to the house. Creeping up to the front door, each man pulled out a ski-mask and put it on to hide their identity. Squatting down under the window on the side of the house, Ren could make out the silhouette of two people sitting on the couch. He turned and motioned to the guys that Dwayne and Jason were to take the front entrance. While him and Manny would enter through the rear.

At the back door, Manny fell to one knee,

pulled out some burglary tools, and began to pick the lock open. Ren went in first pointing his gun and whispered, "Clear," as he secured the kitchen. Manny came in next as they tiptoed towards the living room where they could hear the TV playing. Red and Jamie were sitting on the couch with plates in hand, eating the catfish she prepared.

"We're in," Ren whispered on his radio to Dwayne and Jason, who were standing by the front door waiting for the signal. Ren peeked around the corner to see Jamie heading his way. He quickly ducked back behind the kitchen counter. He watched as she walked down the hallway to the bathroom and shut the door. Ren motioned to Manny to cover the bathroom while he continued to creep into the living room. He pulled out a flashlight and shined it at the window. Dwayne saw the signal, turned and looked at Jason, while nodding his head. He took a step back and with great force used his two hundred and forty pound body to forcefully kick down the front door.

"Don't move!" They all yelled simultaneously.

Red saw the door come crashing down and he scrambled to get his gun that was tucked under one of the pillows on the couch. He pulled out the chrome forty five and aimed it at the first person he saw coming through the door, which was Jason. He had Jason's head in his sights when he felt the cold barrel of Ren's policed issued nine-millimeter pressed against the back of his head.

"Drop it or die!" Ren commanded.

Red dropped the gun immediately. Ren placed his hands behind his back and put on the plastic handcuffs that looked like zip ties.

"What the fuck is going on? Who are you?" Red was yelling, as he squirmed in his restraints.

"Shut up!" Ren ordered.

"Do you guys know who the fuck I am? I'll have your..." and before he could get out another word, Dwayne stuffed a rag in his mouth and taped it shut.

Then the bathroom door open. Manny heard the sound of the toilet flushing as Jamie came out the bathroom saying, "Baby what was that noise?"

As soon as she passed by Manny, he clocked her in the back of the head and knocked her out cold. Manny bent down and checked her.

"Okay let's get outta here," Ren said, as he and Jason grabbed Red and led him out the front door.

Dwayne ran, got the van, and pulled up into the drive way. Manny sprinted up and open the front door. Ren and Jason tossed Red in the back face first. They hopped in after him and sped off.

**

The van pulled into Torch's shop about a

quarter to eleven. Ren was in the van by himself. He didn't want the rest of the Ghost Squad to meet with Torch for the obvious reasons. Torch was standing by one of the bay doors and walked over as Ren stayed seated in the van.

"What you got for me, ese?" Torch asked.

"Exactly what I promised," Ren replied. "He's in the back."

Torch turned to one of his subordinates and nodded his head. Five guys walked to the back of the van and pulled Red out. He was squirming around, but it was no use. Each guy grabbed a limb and took him into one of the empty garages.

"There's just one thing Torch. I don't care what you do to him; just make sure that no one ever finds his body. Understand?"

"You got it homez."

Ren drove off, while Torch followed Red into the garage. They put chains on Red's hands and hung him from a hook they used to pull engines from cars. Torch walked over slowly with a serious look on his face.

"You fucked up when you killed my cousin ese," Torch said ripping the tape off Red's mouth.

"Wait a minute Torch, we can work this out. It's just a misunderstanding. I can give you anything you want, money is no object," Red pleaded in between gasp of breaths.

"Do you know why they call me Torch ese?" He asked totally ignoring Red's pleas.

"Most people think it's because I did body work on cars in my uncle's shop. But that's not why. When I was seventeen this guy named Chico broke into my house and stole a necklace my grandmother gave to me before she died. You see, family is one of the most important things to me. So I had to get that necklace back. I found out who the punk was and tried to get him to give me my grandmother's necklace back. But he refused, so I took him to my uncle's garage. I tied him up and blow torched his hair off until he told me everything I wanted to know," Torched explained while he grabbed a blow torch off the counter.

"Torch please! In God's name don't kill me!"

"God huh? I'll tell you what. I'll give you ten minutes, and if God comes here I'll let you go, deal?" Torch said tapping Red on the face with a sinister smile, "I'll be back."

CHAPTER 18

Keith and Natalie were spooning as they were sound asleep. They both had taken turns feeding and changing the baby all night long. Then around six in the morning the phone rang. Exhausted, Keith rolled over through the jumbled up sheets and answered the phone.

"Hello."

"Keith this is Stanton. We need to talk."

"What the hell are you doing calling me at home?" Keith whispered.

"Meet me at the Walgreens around the corner from your house in thirty minutes," Stanton said before hanging up abruptly.

"Baby who was that?" Natalie inquired while yawning.

"It's the job. Don't worry about it. Go on back to sleep," Keith replied pulling back the sheets and getting out of bed.

"I gotta get up anyway. Nina is coming over to help me with the baby."

Keith went into the bathroom and quickly

got dressed. Irritated by the fact that Stanton called him at his home, he bypassed his morning ritual of eating a bowl of Frosted Flakes and immediately head for his car that was parked out front. Just as he open the front door, Nina had rung the doorbell.

"Nina, what are you doing here so early?"

"Hello to you too. Natalie's mother had a doctor's appointment this morning, so I volunteered to come over and help my girl in her place."

"I'm sorry it's been a rough morning. How are you doing?" He asked giving her a hug and a kiss on the cheek.

"I'm fine."

"Where's Michael?"

"Ren always takes him to school in the morning."

"Oh yeah, what am I thinking. Well I gotta go. Take it easy," he said as he continued to his car.

Keith pulled into the parking lot of the Walgreens moments later. The store was closed and the parking lot was empty. He drove around back and saw Stanton sitting in a gray Lincoln Town car. Walking over, he surveyed the scene several times to make sure that nobody else was around before tapping on the window. Stanton hit the lock on the passenger side door and Keith quickly got in.

"What the hell are you doing calling my house like that!" Keith said angrily.

"We needed to talk. It was either here or at The Ship where everyone can see," Stanton answered.

"What's so important that you had to wake me up at six-something in the morning?"

"Well, I got approval from the D.A's office. You'll get complete transactional immunity for your full cooperation. It's being drawn up as we speak. District Attorney Logan is out of the office until Monday with personal issues. So it'll be signed first thing Monday morning."

Keith turned around and closed his eyes, "I don't know if I can go through with this. Ren's wife, the godmother to my children, just came to my house to help with my baby! Ren and his family have always been there for me. He's like a brother to me. This will hurt him. I don't know if can do that to him," Keith said rubbing on his mustache.

"I don't have time for your flip-flopping. I've been about as patient as I can be with you. Look, that immunity document will be signed on Monday. You have until then to make up your mind, and know this. If you fuck me on this, after I went out on limb for you, I will convene a Grand Jury and indict you on grand larceny and obstruction of justice. I'll subpoena your wife to testify about all your finances and bank records. And if I find out that she's involved in the least, I'll have her arrested and I'll place your children in foster care," Stanton said coldly. "Now, this conversation is over. Get out my damn car."

Keith stared at him for a second, and then slowly got out the car without saying a word. The moment he closed the door, Stanton peeled off and out of sight. Keith looked up at the sky, where the sun was just starting to break through the early morning dew, as if he was looking for a sign from God.

***

At The Ship about an hour later, officers entered the meeting room preparing for roll call. A rookie handed out the updated packets to the rest of the officers. Ren and the Ghost Squad took their seats as Captain Riley made his way up to the podium.

"Okay ladies and gentlemen time to get down to business. The *Hands off Killer* has claimed another victim. Cynthia Morrow, a twenty-nine year old African American woman, was his latest victim. Just like the previous victims, she was murdered in front of her home, and in the same manner."

"Damn!" Ren blurted out.

"Was there something you wanted to add Detective Love?" The Captain asked staring at Ren along with every other policeman who was sitting in the room.

"Ah, no sir," Ren answered quickly.

"As I was saying, we have updated the profile on the killer. It's in your packet, review it closely. Also, on Saturday I've setup several town hall meetings at nearby churches. I want the shift commanders to open a dialogue with the public to try to ease concerns. Each commander will be given a time and location of the meeting they will attend. That's all," the Captain said exiting the room.

Ren and the boys went into the clubhouse. There was a feeling of uneasiness and tension in the room. Keith was still debating in his mind whether or not to spill the beans on his friends. Ren again was bothered by what he saw in his handout. And Jason was on edge knowing that Stanton is putting the squeeze on Keith and not sure how Ren is going to handle it.

"So what do we have going on today?" Dwayne asked breaking the awkward silence as he pulled his gun out of his locker.

"Dwayne, Manny, and Keith I want you guys to get started going through all the open case files for the last six months. Prep the ones that need to go to cold cases and send them downtown when you're finished. Jason and I are going to hit the streets and follow up a couple of leads," Ren said as he and Jason turned and left out through the front door.

They stepped outside and shielded their eyes from the blinding sunlight that was shining in their faces. It was another three digit day, and the humidity was out of control. Jason continued to wear a look of concern on his face as they made their way to Ren's car.

"I know this might not be the right time to talk about this Ren, but now that we got the Red situation under control what about Keith?" Jason asked cracking his knuckles.

"I've been thinking about it. We need to know what Stanton knows. And I think I gotta way we can find out."

"How?"

"Heather told me that he does his work at home. So we're going to get on his computer and access his hard drive, and find the information," Ren said hitting the alarm so that both of them can get into his car.

"What we gonna do, break into the home of an Internal Affairs lieutenant? Our asses will really be in a sling then," Jason chuckled.

"That's exactly what we're going to do, and Heather is going to help us walk right through the front door," Ren replied smiling.

"You're serious aren't you?"

"Dead serious!"

"I don't know if I'm comfortable with this Ren. Breaking into a drug dealer's house is one thing. Breaking into a police officer's house is another."

"C'mon Jason, I need you. You're the only one on the squad that is proficient enough to hack into Stanton's computer terminal. I've already got it setup. In thirty minutes I'll have a little midday rendezvous with Heather at her place. The alarm will be off, I'll unlock the windows, and while I'm busy with her. You can

slip in and out with the information before anyone knows what happened. This will work.
Trust me," Ren said with a reassuring pat on the
shoulder. Once again Ren's charisma and charm
was undeniable as Jason nodded his head in
agreement.

Reading the directions Heather had given
him, Ren navigated his way through a maze of
streets until he found the neighborhood he was
looking for. He wanted to let out Jason away
from the house first and make sure the last minute instructions are clear.

"Okay Jason, once I'm inside I'll unlock the
window. When I get her in the next room I'll
text you the word *go*. Got it," Ren said.

"Yeah, I got it," Jason looking a little on
edge.

They pulled into the new subdivision and
stopped around the corner from the Stanton
house. You could tell that the neighborhood
was being developed because there were still
open lots and a Fox and Jacob's spec-house
with flags flying out front. Jason got out the car
and immediately started making his way down
the alley. Ren continued down the block. He
found the house he was looking for and parked
across the street and two houses down. He
walked up to the Stanton house to see a well
manicured lawn. Ringing the doorbell, he saw
Heather peaking through the curtains.

"Hey there stranger," Heather said opening
the door in a sexy looking satin robe.

Ren quickly stepped in and closed the door. The delightful fragrance of a vanilla scented Glade Plug in's filled the room. Heather's house was immaculate. Being a stay at home wife, the one thing she made sure of is that her house stayed spotless. She had taken over a year to carefully decorate and get her home the exact way she wanted it. Most of her ideas like paint collages, designing a custom made fireplace with polished stones, and ceramic kitchen counter tops came from her favorite TV show *Trading Spaces.*

"Nice place," Ren said taking in the ambiance.

"Thank you, but don't you notice something else," she replied opening her robe to reveal the black laced negligee she was wearing.

"You look stunning," Ren commented as he took a good look at her outfit.

"Thank you. I can't believe you actually came. You don't know how much this excites me," she said rubbing on Ren's dick with a smile that went from ear to ear.

"I know this is what you always wanted. To spice things up even more and you know I'm always eager to please," Ren said kissing her on the neck.

"Just you being here has got me so wet right now. C'mon in here, I want you now," she commanded, grabbing his hand trying to lead him into her bedroom.

"Before we go back there, you mind getting

me a drink? It is pretty hot outside," Ren asked, as he took a look at the lock on the living room window.

On cloud nine for Ren giving into one of her fantasies, she glided into the kitchen to get Ren his water. Ren watched as she left the room and he swiftly went over to the window and unlocked it. He pulled out his phone and started to push in the g-o on his text to send to Jason when.

"Here we go. A nice big glass of juice for a nice big man."

Ren, startled she came back so fast, closed up his cell phone and stuck it in his pocket quickly.

"Everything okay?" She asked handing him a glass of orange juice.

"Yeah, everything is fine. Just a little business," he said smiling and taking a sip of the juice.

She softly grabbed the glass from his hand and set on the table. Taking his right hand, she motioned with her index finger to follow her into the bedroom. Ren followed reluctantly. He knew he had to get the text to Jason or it's all for nothing.

In the bedroom Heather was a tiger. She literally jumped on him as soon as they got into the room. She began to peel off his pants immediately. Normally, this would've been an idealistic situation, there's nothing Ren loves more than a good blow job. But it will be difficult to make a call with his pants on the floor and the phone is inside of them. He tried to stave off the natural enjoyment he was feeling and stay focused, but she was making it hard, the dick I mean. She was giving him a little extra special something, something. She was sucking on that dick, like you would suck on an extra thick milkshake with a thin straw. Ren clinched the sheets as his eyes almost rolled into the back of his head with pleasure. Almost forgetting why he was there in the first place, he finally wiggled loose from her grip after about ten minutes and flipped her over. He slid to the floor on his knees while pulling her to the edge of the bed. She scooted into position as her legs spread faster than butter on hot toast. Ren's tongue gently caressed her sopping wet pussy. She laid back, held her breast, and closed her eyes. Soon as that happen, he began to vigorously search the floor for his pants. He managed to pry loose his cell phone from his front pocket. Never letting his tongue lose contact with the pussy, he punched in the text message and hit send all while Heather was getting her first orgasm.

Jason was outside squatting down in between the house and the air conditioning unit. Beginning to sweat from the intense heat, he had his cell phone in hand waiting for the text message. The chime went off. He got his cue. Walking over to the living room window he gently lifted it. Pushing back the curtains, he slipped through the window with ease. He slowly tip-toed to the hallway to make sure the coast was clear. He looked and saw the door to the room that Ren and Heather were in was slightly cracked. He peaked through to see Ren standing up holding Heather with her legs wrapped around his waist. She's bouncing up and down on his dick like a pogo-stick. He had to cover his mouth to keep from laughing out loud as he heard Heather screaming, "This is your pussy! This is your pussy! This is your pussyyyy!"

Ren saw Jason peaking through the door. With a serious look on his face, he winked and motioned with his eyes for Jason to get back to business. Jason turned around and started searching the rooms for Stanton's workstation. Opening the door to what looked like a home office, he saw the computer, took a seat, and began to reboot it.

Now Jason was a computer expert. It was his first love. His mom brought him a Commadore 64 when he was thirteen and he's been hooked ever since. He majored in computer science at Oklahoma State, where he received his Bachelor's of Science Degree. He was familiar with all kinds of software and could hack into damn near anything. Within a few minutes at the terminal, he had penetrated the firewall, decrypted the files, and gained access to Stanton's personal documents. He went under a heading for *current investigations* and found the file under Keith's name. Pulling a flashdrive out his pocket, he quickly began to download the information. As he closed out that screen another section caught his attention. Curiosity got the best of him as he opened up a heading called two timers and began flipping through the folders. He was stunned to see one with Ren's name on it. He pulled it up and began scanning through it. Horrified by what he saw, Jason decided to down load that information as well. Quickly logging off the computer, he pulled out the flashdrive and put the room back exactly like he found it.

He stepped out into the hallway to hear complete silence. Swiftly, he tip-toed into the living room and over toward the window. This time when he opened the window it made a squeaking sound. He froze like a statue, petrified with fear.

"Did you hear that?" Heather asked sitting up in the bed.

"Hear what?" Ren replied.

"A noise coming from the living room," she said grabbing her robe.

"It's probably nothing," he said trying to calm her down.

"I'm going to see what it is."

Ren scrambled to get his clothes on and stop her, "I'll check for you."

"That's okay," she said walking toward the living room.

Jason heard the voice and her footsteps coming his way. He pushed the window all the

way open and dove through it just before
Heather walked in the room. Ren came running
out zipping his pants up.

"Damn! Did I leave this window open?"

She briskly walked over toward the window.
Jason hitting the soft recently watered grass
hard, heard what Heather said, and rolled
against the house under the window. Heather
stuck her head half way out, looked side to side,
and closed it back shut. Jason let out a big sigh
of relief while clutching his heart like Redd
Foxx from *Sanford and Son*.

"I guess you were right baby. Must've been
nothing," she revealed.

***

After Ren finished with Heather, he picked
up Jason around the corner, and they returned to
The Ship. Once there Ren sent Jason into the
Clubhouse to print up the documents they just
received, while he went into the Captain's office to brief him on current cases.

Jason walked into the Clubhouse to find
Dwayne and Manny packing up boxes and putting them into the storage closet.

"You boys already finish?" Jason asked
grabbing a seat in front of the computer terminal.

"Yeah, it didn't take long. Keith volunteered to run the files downtown for us,"
Manny replied.

"So what leads were you and Ren following up on?" Dwayne asked.

"Nothing much," Jason answered without looking up. His eyes were fixated on the screen as he read what Stanton had written in his confidential notes. It had the detailed information of the CSU reports that showed Keith's fingerprints on the safe. Copies of his financial records, the sign affidavits, even interviews Stanton had conducted with Momo's brother Red were in there. Also, there was a copy of the immunity agreement with Keith's name on it. And the last page had some personal notes.

The district attorney will sign the agreement on Monday morning. Keith seems like he's on the fence, but I have no doubt that he'll sign the immunity agreement with a little push. I'll use his wife's possible involvement with his finances as leverage. I'll meet with him in the morning to discuss.

After reading this, Jason had a sinking feeling in his stomach. He sat back in his chair and began rubbing his hands over his spiked blonde hair.

"I got a feeling you're not telling me something. What's up Jason?" Dwayne asked noticing Jason's weird mannerisms.

"Ren asked me not to say anything until we knew more."

"Knew more about what? What are you talking about?"

The door opened and Ren walked through.

Jason, Manny, and Dwayne got quiet immediately as they looked around at each other.

"What's wrong?" Ren asked.

"Ren I was just looking at the documents. It's worst then we thought. We have to let Manny and Dwayne know what's going on," Jason replied.

He walked over to Jason and extended his hand, "Let me see what you got." He read through everything with a blank expression as the rest of the boys looked on. He sighed and then handed the material to Dwayne.

"Holy shit!" Dwayne blurted out as he handed the file to Manny.

"Why didn't you tell us about this, Ren?"

"Because I didn't want any over reactions until I knew exactly what we're dealing with?"

"What we're dealing with is a motherfucka that's about to rat us out to Internal Affairs!" Dwayne added.

"He's right Ren. We should have known about this the moment you did," Manny stated calmly.

"Fuck all that! He's going to sign that agreement come Monday morning. So what are we gonna do now?" Jason asked standing up

"It's obvious. We have to stop him at any cost," Manny commented.

"I agree," Dwayne added.

"So do I," Jason said also.

"Wait a minute, wait a minute. Everybody needs to just calm the fuck down."

"C'mon Ren, you know what needs to be done here. What's your motto, *no loose ends.* Well, this end is loose like a motherfucka, and needs to be tighten up quickly," Jason retorted.

"Hold up! Keith is a member of this squad and my best friend. I've known the man for over thirty years. I just stood godfather to his newborn child and you think I'm gonna fucking clip him. Please! He's just under tremendous pressure, and he feels like he has no one to turn to. I got a fishing trip planned for Saturday. I'll talk to him. Once he finds out that we have his back, he'll keep his mouth shut. Trust me," Ren said, angrily.

The guys looked around at each other, and then Jason stepped forward as if they secretly name him the official spokesman. "Today is Friday; you got until Sunday to talk to him Ren. But if we're not reassured that Keith is on our team, we will have to resort to drastic measures."

"We'll see about that!" Ren responded sharply as he turned and left the room. Jason went back over to the computer and grabbed some more pages that were still on the printer. He ran back out the door to catch up with Ren.

"Ren," Jason said grabbing at his arm.

"What!"

"There is something else that I found on Stanton's computer. Something on a more personal note," Jason whispered with eyes darting back and forth.

"What is it? Spit it out!" Ren commanded.

"Step over here," Jason replied as Ren followed him into the vacant hallway. "I didn't want to say anything in front of the other guys, but Stanton knows about you and Heather," Jason said handing him the notes from Stanton's computer, "Apparently he's had a private eye following you for awhile. According to the documents, the first contact with him was in May. That's way before Momo bit the bullet. There are even pictures from the hotel rooms you've been in. You were right. He does have an axe to grind with you."

Ren scan through the information, rolled up the papers, placed them in his back pocket and said, "I don't have time for this shit right now! I'll deal with it later," he snapped. Dejected from the Keith situation, he turned and left out the glass doors to the parking lot without saying another word.

CHAPTER 19

Stanton walked through the door of his home around a quarter to ten on Friday night. Setting down his briefcase next to the couch, he took off his suit coat and tossed it on the armchair in the living room. Loosening up his tie, he slowly made his way to the bedroom. He saw Heather lying on her side of the bed curled into a fetal position reading a book called *Chicken Soup to Inspire a Woman's Soul*. She had on a pair of cutoff shorts that showed her camel toe and an old wife-beater shirt. Having just stepped out the shower minutes before Stanton had arrived, the little sprinkles of water on her back combined with the ceiling fan running made her nipples sprout out. She had thoroughly oiled down her body and was glistening under the ceiling-fan lights she was using to read.

"Hey," Stanton said getting undressed, "How was your day?"

"Fine," Heather replied dryly.

Stanton had quickly stripped down to his

underwear. He stood on his side of the bed admiring his wife from behind. It's been a long three months since the last time they made love, and just the thought of caressing his wife's supple skin began to make his nature rise. She looked so sexy and inviting to him. Lying down next to Heather he rested his head on her hip and gently reached down to touch her feet. She had a pedicure earlier in the day and the pink nail polish was really setting off her creamy bright skin.

"Quit!" She screamed.

"What's the problem?" He asked with a hint of frustration in his voice.

"I'm not in the mood for that," she replied pushing his hand away.

"C'mon baby," he pleaded trying to scoot up behind her. So that she could feel that he was fully aroused.

"No! I'm not in the mood."

"I'm sick of this shit!" He yelled, "Every night it's the same damn thing. You're my wife and I want some loving!"

"Like I told you, I'm not in the mood for all that! Now leave me alone," she said pushing him off her.

Stanton stood up and with fire in his eyes said, "Oh you can't make love to me, but you can spend time with that motherfucker Ren!"

Heather was astonished at this revelation. Almost immediately she got that gut wrenching feeling in the pit of her stomach. Never in her wildest imagination did she ever think that Stanton would find out. She and Ren had taken every necessary precaution, today's events aside. Closing her book, Heather looked up at Stanton and without flinching said, "I have no idea what you're talking about."

"Yes you do. You see I've had a private eye following you for the last four months. I even have pictures of your rendezvous at the Howard Johnson. It seems you always get the same room, 456. Sound familiar? I know everything, so don't try to deny it. Don't you dare try to deny it! I only have one question," then he paused for a second, "Why?" He asked with a stone face.

"You really wanna know why, huh Greg?" She questioned putting the book on the night-stand and sitting up on the edge of the bed.

"Yeah! I've been a good husband. I've been faithful to you. I work hard every day to put a roof over your head. I think I deserve some answers."

"Fine! You're right Greg, I have been seeing Ren. I won't deny it. Ren, unlike you, he has time for me! He listens to what I have to say. He cares about my feelings."

"What are you talking about Heather? I listen, I care about your feelings," he replied.

"No you don't. Your head is so buried in your work, that you haven't heard one word I said in years. I haven't mattered in your life for a long time. I'm just a trophy you show off to your friends at banquets and social functions. Someone to clean your house, and give you sex when you need it. Your career comes before me. That's what you really care about. That's the most important thing to you. Spending time with me is a distant second, and I'm tired of coming in second."

Stanton looked down at the floor. He was furious. "So you think fucking another man is the answer?"

"No! I didn't go out looking for it. It just happened. But if you had been there for me, there would've been no opportunity for him to move in."

Stanton shook his head. He went into the closet and pulled out a suitcase. Walking over to the other side of the bed he slammed it down and unzipped it. Yanking open the dresser draws, he began to throw his clothes into a suitcase.

"What are you doing?" She asked him.

"I'm getting the hell out of here! I can't stand to look at your face another second," he replied.

"Wait a minute, we need to finish talking about this," she pleaded reaching for his arm.

"You disgust me you little whore," he twisted a loose from her grip. "I never wanna see you again," he said grabbing a few more of his things and then heading for the front door.

Heather quickly raced to beat him to the front door. She stood in front of it with her arms and legs spread trying to keep him from walking out. "You're not going anywhere. Not till we finish talking about this."

He pushed her light hundred and ten pound frame to the ground. "We have nothing to talk about," he said coldly opening the door, "You and your little boyfriend are going to get what's coming to you! Believe that, bitch." Then he slammed the door with so much fury, that several pictures fell from the walls.

Heather crawled into the corner breathing hard. She buried her face into her folded arms and began bawling like a newborn baby. The years of frustration came pouring out with every tear. Curling into a ball, she rocked back and forth just letting the tears flow continuously down her soft cheeks. After a few minutes passed, she rose to her feet and went to the bathroom to get some tissue. She blew her nose and wiped the tears from her watery eyes. Going back into the bedroom, she pulled back the sheets and climbed into bed.

***

Several hours later, a weird sound woke Heather up out of a light sleep. She took the pillow off her head and wiped the matter from her eyes and looked at the clock on the wall. It was three in the morning. Standing up slowly, she walked over to the blinds and peaked out the window, but nothing was there. She walked to the front door and cracked it slowly. She stepped outside into the warm night air. Temperatures earlier in the day had reached over a hundred, but now it had cooled off substantially. It just so happen to be a full moon this night and the sky was clear. It was one of those rare nights in the city where you could actually see all the stars.

Turning on the porch light, she carefully stepped outside and walked around to the side of the house where the noise was coming from. The fan on the air conditioning unit was blowing. Then out of nowhere a cat jumped out of the bushes. Heather was startled as she jumped back with fear. She laughed it off when she saw it was only a stray cat. Ready to go back inside the friendly confines of her home, Heather felt a strange presence in her mist. A tingling sensation came over her all of a sudden. She turned around to see a mysterious figure dressed in all black. She moved closer and recognized the face, "Oh it's just you. You scared me. What are you doing out here this time of night?"

"Looking for you," the person murmured. And without warning a blade came seemingly out of nowhere to slash Heather right across her throat.

She fell to the ground holding her throat and gasping for air. "Please, please don't kill me," she struggled to say grabbing her neck trying to stop the blood that was gushing out.

The mysterious figure squatted down on one

knee and grabbed the helpless Heather by the top of her hair, and took one more swipe at the back of her neck. She continued choking and coughing trying desperately to breathe, but it was of no use. The cuts were too deep. She took her last gasp as her bloody body laid there lifeless.

CHAPTER 20

The best time to go fishing is early in the morning, the earlier the better. So Ren picked up Keith around 4am, and they headed over to Joe Pool Lake on the southern outskirts of Dallas. The lake is located in a state park so they had to pay the five dollar fee at the entrance gate to get in. Driving down the twisted-gravel-paved-road that was surrounded by trees, they made their way down to the boat dock where Ren paid a nominal fee to park his boat. His boat, which he called Billie Holiday after the late blues singer, was a top of the line 270 Mackinaw. Normally, a fine boat like this would run over a hundred grand, but Ren got a great deal as he bought it off the widow of a fisherman who died last year for half price.

Ren pulled out of his trunk a picnic basket that contained some sandwiches that Nina had packed for him. He grabbed it along with his fishing poles and tackle-box. Keith grabbed the cooler which was half filled with bait, and the other half filled with cold Coor's light. They carried all their stuff down the long dock and aboard the boat. Ren untied the rope holding the boat in place and started the engines.

"Hold up a second Ren. I don't see the life jackets."

Ren looked around for a second to see if he could find them. "Damn it! I forgot that I let Old man Allen use them when he went out the other day. He must've forgotten to put them back when he was finished," he replied.

"So, are we gonna sit here and wait for him or what? 'Cause you know I ain't getting on no boat without it, bad a swimmer as I am," Keith asked.

"There's no telling when the old man will show up, if at all. Look, we're already out here. I'll take it slow. We won't even go out that far on the water."

"You'll take it slow?" Keith asked.

"Of course. C'mon, we've been out hundreds of times and you've never fallen overboard yet. Trust me," Ren said with pleading eyes.

"Okay," Keith answered as he pulled up the anchor.

They were the only ones out on the lake so far. The sun hadn't fully risen yet. It was fighting its way through the early morning cloud coverage. Stepping inside the cockpit and taking a seat in his captain's chair, Ren hit the throttle fast as he customarily does and they zipped away from the shore. The water was calm as the boat seemed to glide effortlessly across the lake's surface until the dock almost disappeared from view. They finally came to a stop about a mile out. They opened the cooler, pulled out their bait, and began prepping their lines to cast into the water. Settling into the chairs in the back of the boat, Ren and Keith crack opened a couple of beers and kicked their feet up.

At first there was a long awkward silence. You're not supposed to be doing too much loud talking this time of morning anyway because you could possibly scare the fish away. But Ren and Keith weren't even looking at each other at first. Finally, Keith broke the silence.

"You know Zakiea slept all the way through the night for the first time."

"Oh yeah!"

"Yeah. I haven't slept that good in over a month. And just so happens that the night I get a full nights sleep is the night I had one of the weirdest dreams."

"What about?" Ren inquired.

"I was driving in my car by myself. I had to change freeways. So I went over one of those huge overpasses. You know what I'm talking about, one those big mix masters with the multiple bridges. When I first looked at it, it was fine. Then when I got to the very top, half of the bridge was missing. Only I didn't notice until it was too late. I went over the edge and before I hit the ground, I woke up. What you think that means?" Keith asked curiously.

"They say dreams are your subconscious mind speaking to you. So the answer to what it means is in you, I guess," Ren replied.

"Hmm. I guess you're right. Do you ever have dreams like that?"

"Nah, I don't dream about shit," Ren said polishing off his beer and tossing it in the trash.

"You mind if I ask you a question?"

"Shoot," Ren replied.

"Why did you become a policeman?"

Ren sat back in his chair. He cleared his throat and looked up at the sky, "It's funny you should mention that. With everything that's been going on lately, I've actually though about it. I remember being in the Commandant's office at the police academy when he asked me that very question before approving me for enlistment. I said something generic about making a big difference. And he told me something I'll never forget. He said, "Son, making a difference is for Superman. So if you wanna be a hero join the fire department. Being a policeman is about one thing, keeping order." At the time I had no idea what the hell that man was talking about. It wasn't until seven years later when I first made detective that I understood. I was working vice and there was this pimp name Monroe. Monroe had a stable full of the finest hoes in Dallas. They worked this one corner on Harry Hines Blvd. I had gotten multiple complaints from business owners about his hoes tricking in front of their establishments. The smart thing to do would have been to push them over a couple of blocks. But I let Monroe get under my skin. I was determined to take him down. To make a long story short, I eventually caught Monroe slipping and busted him. And when I did, his hoes had no more guidance. They started turning tricks everywhere including schools, drifting into the wrong neighborhoods, getting high. One of them was beaten to death by some Jon in his car. Others became homeless. It was a big mess. At the end of the day, when I step back and looked at the big picture, as ugly as it was, Monroe had his place in keeping order on the streets. And busting him only disrupted the natural balance of things. It was then that I understood what the Commandant was talking about. That sometimes keeping order might mean that you have to give some people a pass. So to answer your question, keeping the order," Ren said opening another bottle of beer and taking a swig.

"C'mon Ren, I know you better than that. You're the one that convinced me of joining the force, remember? You were the president of *The Future Leaders of America* back in college. And you had all these great ideas about how you wanted to change the world. That we were gonna go back to Pleasant Grove after we graduate and clean up the community, remember that?" Keith stated.

"Yeah....that was a long time ago," Ren said

leaning back with a strange smirk, "Before I knew the truth of just how shitty this world can be. You see you're an optimist Keith, that's why I love ya bro. You're an affable guy looking for the best in everything. Me, I'm a realist. When I look at a half of glass of water, I don't see it as half full or half empty. To me, it's just a half of glass of fucking water. Changing the world, shit, they ain't made enough prisons to accomplish that feat."

Keith hung his head low, "I'm sorry you feel that way."

Ren sat his drink down. He took his fishing-pole and hooked it to a brace so that he didn't have to take his line out the water. Taking a deep breath, he locked eyes with Keith. "I know where this conversation is going."

"What are you talking about?" Keith responded.

"I know that Stanton is putting the squeeze on you."

"What?" Keith said completely dumbfounded.

"I know everything. How he threaten Natalie and the kids, your fingerprints on the safe, and the deal he's offering you. Everything!"

Keith's mouth was moving, but no words came out. He stood up and dropped his pole, then finally collected his thoughts. "How did you find out?"

"The hard way, but I should've found out from you. We're brothers. You should've come to me first."

"The rest of the guys know about this?" Keith asked turning away from Ren.

"Yeah," Ren answered.

"Ah shit!" Keith yelled in frustration hitting the arm of the chair.

"Just calm down. I got those guys under control. You don't gotta worry about them. Now I know you haven't told him nothing yet, or I'd be wearing handcuffs. So we still have a chance to clean this mess up before it's too late."

"No Ren!" Keith said interrupting, "I can't clean this up or sweep it under some rug. I'm tired. I'm tired of lying. I'm tired of sleepless nights. I'm tired of the moral dilemma that I have to wrestle with on a daily basis. I just want some peace of mind."

"And I'll give it to you. I got some strings I can pull to make this go away. I'm just gonna need your help. Trust me," Ren retorted.

"This is so typical of you. To sweet talk me into doing what you want. You didn't listen to me at all. But then it's never been about me, has it Ren? My whole life I spent walking in the footsteps of the great Lorenzo Love. I went to LSU because you went there. I got a degree in criminal justice because you did. I became a cop because you thought it was the best thing to do. It wasn't my idea to kill Momo and take his money, it was yours. And now my life is being turned upside down because of it," Keith yelled. "For once, just once, have you ever considered what I want? I've always had your back, why don't you have mines for once. Tell Stanton the truth and stop letting me twist in the damn wind," Keith yelled at the top of his voice as the tears began rolling down his cheeks.

"I didn't know you felt that way," Ren said stepping closer to Keith and hugging him tightly. "I'm sorry. I never wanted to hurt you. I love you man. You're my inspiration. You're my brother. If turning myself in can make this right, so be it."

"For real?" Keith murmured with his eyes widening.

"Of course. I got your back."

Ren turned Keith loose as he wiped the tears from his eyes. Ren walked back over to his fishing pole and reeled in the line. "Let's get outta here."

"Okay," Keith replied with a look of relief.

Ren walked back to the cockpit with Keith behind him. Ren sat down in his captain's seat and turned back on the engine. Keith realizing he left his pole with the line in the water ran back to pull it out. Not noticing or hearing Keith walking to the back of the ship because of the loud roar of the engines, Ren put the boat in gear and hit the throttle. Keith got to the seat he was sitting in and bent over to pickup his fishing pole when Ren hit the throttle. The sudden take-off caused Keith's momentum to carry him off the back of the boat and into the water.

After hitting the throttle Ren turned around and didn't see Keith. Bringing the boat to a grinding stop, Ren ran to the back to see what happened. With no life jacket, Keith was struggling to keep his head above water. His feeble attempts to tread water are useless though.

"Hold on Keith!" Ren yelled out as he scrambled to get the life preserver.

Grabbing the white life preserver from the hook, he quickly went back over to where Keith was at. He was continuing to struggle staying above the water as he cried out with water filled lungs, "Help, help!"

Ren rushed over ready to throw the life preserver into the water, then it seemed for a second as if time stood still. He froze like a Greek statue. The future flashed before his very eyes, staring him in the face like his own reflection. The thought of going to prison entered his mind for the first time ever. A life behind bars without family was the fate for him and the Ghost squad. All this went through his mind in a split second. Then it became obvious. As much as he wanted to, his arm wouldn't allow him to throw that life preserver into the water. A golden opportunity had presented itself, and he couldn't ignore it. Standing there still unable to move, he watched as Keith stuck his head above the water for one last gasp of air before he went under permanently.

"I'm sorry!" Ren yelled out as he fell backwards on to the ship's deck with his face in his hands. Seconds later Keith's lifeless body floated back to the surface faced down. And for the first time since his mother passed away, tears began to roll down Ren's cheeks.

CHAPTER 21

Jeff started his postal route at the usually time, 8 a.m. It was his turn on the rotation to work on the weekend. And as much as he liked the overtime, he was still a little agitated for having to work on a Saturday. He had plans on taking the kids to Sixflags. So, he planned to work as fast as he could to get off at a decent time.

He pulled up to the third mailbox on his route. It was the new kind of mailbox that was steel and contained all the boxes for everyone on the street. Pulling out his keys, he quickly opened the large door and began putting mail into each individual slot. That's when he noticed that the house in front of him had its door cracked open. His eyes surveyed the area and he saw something on the ground in between the houses. Jeff ignored it at first, he continued filling in the mailboxes with there bills, circulars, and personal correspondence.

As he finished and locked back up the box, he glanced over at the house again. Normally as a mailman he sees strange things all the time, but something about this scene didn't set right with him. No longer able to fight off his curiosity, he sat his mailbag down in his truck and went over to investigate. As he got closer in the yard he could make out that it was a woman lying on the ground. He rushed over.

"Are you okay," he said falling to one knee. But there was no answer. He touched the body and it was cold as ice. When he turned the woman over he could see the cut marks on her neck and the pool of blood that had been soaked up by the ground.

"Oh my God!" Jeff whipped out his cell phone and immediately called 911.

Police arrived at the scene quickly. Once the details of the crime scene were reported in, it was obvious that the crime was linked to the *Hands off Killer*. The Ship was contacted and McCain and Bernstein were notified immediately. The leads from the other murders they were working on were coming up dry. And as much as they hated to admit, a fresh murder might drum up new clues.

McCain made his way through the yellow tape as Bernstein followed closely behind. They looked around at the house and sidewalk but nothing jumped out as being significant other than the cracked door. Walking up to the body they saw a familiar site. A woman with her throat cut and the hands cut off. McCain and Bernstein both put on latex gloves as they began to examine the victim's wounds. Bernstein felt her body and noticed how cold she was, while McCain gently ran his fingers across the cuts on her neck.

"You got an ID yet?" McCain asked the young white officer who was first at the scene.

"No sir. I only secured the area. I didn't want to contaminate your crime scene. I thought it would be best if detectives went into the house first," the young officer replied.

"Okay, good job. Why don't you call in and find out who's the owner of record of this house," McCain ordered.

"Yes sir."

McCain knelt down carefully slipped off her house shoes to find another little folded message tucked inside.

"*The Hands that touch me will never touch another,*" were the familiar words typed across the front of the paper. McCain looked in the corner and saw another fresh set of numbers, 8479. He handed the paper to Bernstein who looked over it in amazement.

"It probably won't matter, but have it checked for prints anyway. Maybe we'll get lucky," McCain said standing back up.

"Sure," Bernstein replied turning toward the head of the CSU team that was walking up. "See what you guys can do with this," he said putting the note into a baggy and handing it over.

They walked over to the house and went through the cracked door. Looking around carefully and paying close attention to every detail that was in the home, they went from room to room searching for anything out of the ordinary. After securing the front rooms, McCain took the office while Bernstein checked out the Master bedroom.

Bernstein spotting a purse on the dresser opened it up and found a driver's license. "We got a winner!" He yelled out holding up the ID. "It looks like our victim's is twenty-nine year old Heather Stanton," Bernstein continued.

McCain walked into the bedroom where Bernstein was with a grim look on his face holding a picture. "Look at this," he said handing it over to Bernstein. "Recognize the man in the picture?"

"He looks familiar, who is he?"

"It's Greg Stanton of Internal Affairs."

"You're shittin me?"

"I'm afraid not. I only recognize him because he's been working on a case at The Ship for the past month," McCain responded.

"Ah shit! As if we didn't need to add further insult to injury. Now we have the dead wife of a cop mixed in with this. Wait till the papers get a hold of this. The chief will be livid. We'd better find Greg as soon as possible," Bernstein said.

"So what are you thinking? That he's a suspect?" McCain asked with a curious expression.

"I'm looking at a dead wife, and judging by

her body temperature, she's been dead since last night. There was no forced entry into the home. And a missing husband. Shit, you ain't got to be Sherlock Holmes to figure this one out."

"I don't know," McCain said rubbing his jaw. "It's hard for me to believe he's the *Hands off Killer*. There's no apparent connection to the other women. There's only been one common denominator in every murder, and that's our John Doe. For all we know, this scene could've been staged. And that note might be phony."

"We'll see when the Medical Examiner gets here."

Joan arrived at the scene a few minutes later. She had gotten caught in rush hour traffic, and made the normally punctual Examiner arrive late. Soon as she arrived, she immediately began to examine Heather Stanton. After her field examination of the victim, she was convinced that the wounds inflicted on Heather were consistent with the previous victims. There was absolutely no doubt in her mind that the same weapon was used to murder all four women. Upon hearing the news, McCain could do nothing but close his eyes and cringe. He knew that Stanton would have to be considered a suspect under these circumstances.

***

Back at The Ship, the two men began the furious search to find Greg Stanton. He wasn't due into work until Monday morning, but McCain knew that the sooner they got him in and question him, the better. Most crimes are solved within twenty-four hours after they're committed. The longer time passes, the fuzzier the details get. So they brewed a pot coffee, rolled up their sleeves and started working the phones. They called all of his local relatives and friends that were in his phone book first, but no one knew where he was at. As they began contacting Stanton's colleagues, the mood at The Ship quickly started to change. People started gathering in circles talking. You could hear noses sniffling, and see tears pouring. Captain Riley walked out of his office with a stoic look. He cleared his throat. "Everyone can I have your attention, please!"

Immediately, all work ceased. There were no more papers rattling. No more keys being hit on computers. A uniform cop tapped on the clubhouse door. Normally, the Ghost Squad was off on the weekend, but Jason and Manny just happened to be there working a couple of angles on a new case.

"I just received some disturbing news," the Captain said then paused for a second. "Detective Keith Sanders accidentally fell off a boat while fishing and drowned. Detective Sanders was a great cop and an even better man. He will be missed. The department psychiatrist will be available to anyone that needs counseling," the Captain announced as he slowly turned around with slumping shoulders and headed back to his office.

There were a lot of long faces and pats on the back as the room cleared. McCain sat back in his chair in utter disbelief. He was no fan of the Ghost Squad and their tactics, but he had always got along with Keith and had mutual respect for any man or woman that wore a shield. It was part of the unwritten code. Jason and Manny looked at each other with shock at first. One of their own had fallen, but his death brought them resolution. Both men secretly breathed a deep sigh of relief.

***

After feeding and changing the baby, Natalie laid down and dozed off for a few minutes. She was extremely tired. Saturday was her cleaning day, and since Keith had his fishing trip this morning, she had to juggle her chores along with taking care of the baby. She didn't bother walking back upstairs to get into her bed. As soon as she finished burping Zakiea, she just put the baby back in her playpen, and crashed out right on the couch. No sooner does Natalie get her eyes closed, when the doorbell rings. She gets up, closed up her robe tightly, and answered the front door.

"Who is it?" She asked wiping those big round eyes of hers.

"It's me big momma," Nina answered, as

Natalie could see her eye staring back at her through the peephole.

"Girl, your timing is bad today," Natalie said opening the door. Nina walked through with Michael closely behind her.

"What's wrong?"

"I just got Zakiea settled down and was about to take me a nap."

"Oh I'm sorry honey. I tell you what, why don't I watch the baby for you while you go upstairs and rest. I'll fix the boys some breakfast too and keep them out of your hair."

"You will?"

"Of course, now go on upstairs," Nina said kissing Natalie on the cheek and turning her around and pushing her toward the stairwell. "I got this covered."

Barely able to keep her eyes open, Natalie was in no position to refuse. She headed to her room while Nina went to the kitchen and commenced to whip up some breakfast. In no time flat she had the boy's plates on the table. They grabbed the jelly and started throwing down on the grits, eggs, sausage, and toast that she piled on their plates. After the boys cleaned their plates, she turned on cartoons for them in the living room while she made her way over to the playpen and picked up the baby. Nina knew she would be spoiling her, but she couldn't help it. Zakiea was so pretty and such a nice baby, that she had to hold her. Nina showered her with affection as she cradled her in her arms. Then the doorbell rang. Instead of waking up Natalie, Nina decided to answer the door herself. She looked through the peephole and saw Ren.

"Hey baby," she said giving him a kiss while still holding the baby. "Look at your god-daughter, isn't she so beautiful?" Nina said with a big smile planting another kiss on her soft chocolate skin. "C'mon on in here and hold her."

Nina hadn't noticed the somber look on Ren's face as she handed him the baby when he stepped inside. He reluctantly took Zakiea as he struggled to get a word in between the praises Nina was giving Zakiea.

"I came over this morning to give Natalie a hand. I knew her mom would be out of town today."

"Nina," Ren tried to interject.

"That poor child looks so burnt out. She could sleep for days," she said basically ignoring him.

"Nina!"

"Keith should've never gone on that fishing trip with you. He should be here helping his wife take care of this precious baby," she said tickling her on her feet.

"Nina!"

"By the way, where is Keith?" she asked.

"Nina!" Ren raised his voice a bit louder until Nina finally got the picture and shut up. "I got something important I need to tell you."

"What's wrong baby?" She asked with

concern on her face, as now Ren has her undivided attention.

"Where is Natalie?"

"She's upstairs getting in a nap while I watched the kids."

Ren cleared his throat and looked up at the ceiling. "There was an accident on the lake while me and Keith went fishing."

"Is he going to be alright?"

Ren shook his head. "No…..he's dead."

"Oh my God! What happened?"

"He fell overboard while reaching for his fishing pole and drowned."

"That's terrible!" Nina cried.

"What's terrible?" Natalie asked walking down the stairs.

Ren and Nina looked at each other nervously. From the looks on their faces Natalie immediately knew that something wasn't right.

"What's wrong? And where's Keith, Ren?" Natalie asked again.

"I think you better sit down," Ren finally responded after a minute or so.

"What the hell I need to sit down for? Just tell me what's going on, and where's my husband at?"

"There was an accident when we were at the lake," Ren said.

Nina touched Ren on the arm to signify she'll take it from here. She walked over to Natalie, put her hands on her shoulders, and locked eyes with her. "Sweetie, Keith fell overboard while they were fishing…..... he drowned."

Natalie stood there for a second while her eyes darted back and forth between Nina and Ren. Then she started to bust out in laughter. "You guys almost had me there for a second. Keith dead, right," Natalie joked while pulling back the curtains. "Where's he at, hiding outside or something?"

Nina grabbed Natalie by the arm and shook her to get her attention, "It's not a joke sweetie. Keith is dead. He's gone!"

"My God you're serious!" Natalie said falling backwards on the couch in disbelief. She closed her eyes tightly and bit down on her balled up fist. Nina sat down next to her and wrapped her arms around her as they both started to cry together. Ren stood there with the baby still in his arms looking at the two women crying on each other's shoulders. The rush of emotions woke the baby out of her light slumber. As she squirmed around in his arms like a fish out of water, he held her closely looking into her eyes and for an instant he saw a flash of Keith's face. In that few seconds he wrestled with the idea of telling the ladies the truth. Ren stepped closer as Natalie grabbed some Kleenex from the coffee table and blew her nose.

"Natalie, I'm so sorry. I tried to save'em, but ah, ah," Ren murmured.

"It's okay Ren. I know you did everything you could," Natalie replied.

"Yeah. You know if I could trade places

with him I would," Ren said as he handed the baby back to Nina, and then gave Natalie a hug. "If there's anything I can do, anything at all, just let me know."

***

Later that night everyone from The Ship gathered at Johnny's bar to pay tribute to Keith. Johnny's was kind of like the unofficial meeting place where cops have their wakes. They would cover the pool table with linen and place the dead body on it. A picture of the cop dressed in their dress blues was placed next to them. Everyone would get up and take turns making speeches and giving toast.

Ren arrived at ten o'clock. He pulled into the parking lot playing Keith's favorite song by Al Green, *Thanks for the Good Times*. Turning off the ignition, he sat there with his hands on the steering wheel listening to the last few verses. As smooth as Al's voice was, he could bring no solace to Ren's aching heart. Slamming the door of his car, he was still feeling the pain from holding Keith's daughter in his hands and having to tell his wife the bad news about her husband. He walked up to see Manny, Dwayne, and Jason all standing out front under a dimly lit corner of the building with long faces. They were huddle up having a conversation when Jason saw Ren approaching. He walked up not saying a word, like his mouth was glued shut.

"How are you doing Ren?" Jason inquired.

"How you think I'm doing?" He answered sarcastically.

"What happened out there with Keith? All we know is what the Captain said, which was very generic," Manny asked.

"What fucking difference does it make, he's gone! You guys got your wish. You finally got what you wanted. Keith is no longer a loose end to you. The one fucking man with more character and conviction than anyone here is no longer a liability. So go inside, drink until your heart's content, and breathe a sigh of relief 'cause you don't have to worry about him ratting you out any more," Ren said with venom in his voice, and fire in his eyes.

"Ren it's not like that. We just ah," Dwayne stammered trying to smooth things over.

"Yeah, I know. You just wanted to save your own ass!" Ren snapped as he turned away to enter the front door.

"Ren!" Jason called out, "Ren please! I need to talk to you for a second."

"What!" Ren answered completely agitated.

Jason caught up to Ren just before he opened the door. He started scratching the back of his head as he searched for the words to say. "Ren, ah, there's something else. It's Heather."

"What about her?"

"I don't know how to tell you this."

"Tell me what? Spit it out!"

"She's dead."

"Dead?" Ren replied in stunning disbelief.

"Yeah, it happened last night. Apparently, she was murdered by the *Hands off Killer.* McCain and this new guy he's working with named Bernstein are looking at her husband as a suspect. They're searching to question him, but haven't found him yet," Jason replied.

"That son-of-a-bitch! How much you wanna bet that that fucker charged her up about the affair," Ren said breathing heavily. "I want that bastard found! You hear me! I want you guys on the street tracking down every lead until he's found! Now!" Ren commanded.

"What about our involvement? McCain is going to have CSU dust that house for fingerprints, and when they do, they're going to find our prints all over the place. How the hell are we going to explain breaking into Stanton's house? Not to mention the fact that you were having an affair with Heather," Jason asked.

"That's why we gotta find him first. Keep the focus on Stanton. Besides, forensics won't think about matching fingerprints against officers without probable cause first. Only thing I have to worry about is those photos on his computer which you said are encrypted. Hopefully by the time they crack it, we'll have Stanton in custody with a full confession and it won't matter," Ren answered as he turned and entered the bar.

Johnny's was packed. It was standing room

only. Every man and woman from The Ship was in attendance. They had a picture of Keith in his dress uniform on the bar for all to see. The guys were climbing on a wooden chair in the middle of the room as they gave short speeches in remembrance. As soon as Ren walked in he was immediately allowed to take the floor as the room fell silent. One of his fellow cops handed him a beer as Ren stood on top of a chair clearing his throat.

"By now everybody in here has heard that I was with Keith when he passed away. I've seen a lot of horrible things on the streets in my twenty years as a cop, but nothing as bad as seeing my best friend drown. I appreciate everyone's support. Keith Sanders was like a brother to me and he'll be missed," Ren said raising his glass for a toast. "To Keith."

"To Keith!" Everyone else repeated in unison as they banged their glasses and mugs against each other and taking big gulps of beer. Then everyone puts their arms around the shoulder of the man next to him, swayed back and forth, and joined in singing *Oh Danny Boy*. That was the traditional Irish song sung at the bar any time a cop dies. By the time the song was done there wasn't a dry eye in the house.

CHAPTER 22

Ren pulled into the underground parking garage of a Downtown law firm. Brian was already there nervously biting his fingernails down to the nub. The garage was dimly lit as Ren looked for a place to park. Killing the engine, Ren got out his car, slammed the door, and carefully surveyed the scene before proceeding. They both walked over behind a large pillar that shields them from any on coming traffic.

"You got what I come here for?" Ren asked.

"Of course, you got the money?" Brian replied.

"Yeah. Let's see the check first."

Brian reached into the small of his back and pulled out a brown envelop and handed it to Ren. Taking the package from him, Ren opened it up and saw a crisp new check for a hundred grand from the Martin & Stevenson Finance company. Putting the check up to the closest light source near them, Ren examined the check closely to make sure it wasn't a forgery.

"It's legit," Brian commented as he watched Ren. "My guys are professionals with a reputation to uphold."

"Just making sure," Ren said handing Brian a small pouch.

Brian unzipped it to find ten stacks of hundreds marked ten thousand dollars a piece. He thumbed through it quickly and closed the bag back up. "I guess our business is finished."

"Certainly is. I'll see you later," Ren said.

"No, I don't think so. My obligation to you is done. I prefer not to hear from you again. Goodbye," Brian said turning and walking back to his car.

Ren left the parking garage and went to the hospice to visit his father. Sundays are the days he prefers the most. It's quiet and more peaceful. No kids running up and down the halls making a bunch of noise. It's usually much more laid back on a Sunday. He walked down through the lobby and into his father's room. Walking in, he sees Dr. Taylor leaning over his father and checking his vital signs.

"I didn't know that doctors made house calls on the weekends," Ren joked as he walked in.

Dr. Taylor turned around with a stone face and said in a solemn tone, "Can I have a word with you in the hallway Mr. Love?"

Ren looked over and saw his father lying there with his eyes closed. "Yeah, okay," Ren said reluctantly as he followed him into the hallway.

"Mr. Love I was called here because your father's condition has gotten worse," Dr. Taylor said.

"It's all right, everything is gonna be fine now. I have the money for the operation," he reached into his pocket and pulled out the check. "See! I'm gonna deposit it first thing Monday morning. So now he can get the operation."

"I'm sorry to have to tell you this Mr. Love, but your father is beyond that point now. It's too late."

Ren looked as if he was dazed for a second, then he grabbed the doctor by the coat and pushed him against the wall. The anger that had been building up inside of him since Keith died was finally starting to overflow.

"What the fuck you mean it's too late? Huh? I got the money! You got any idea what I had to go through to get this money? You have any idea of the lives that were affected so I could get this fucking money? Now you're telling me you can't save my father! The only parent I got left! You telling me everything I've done has been in vein. Huh, huh? That it's too late!" Ren yelled.

Dr. Taylor cowering in fear was kicking his feet that were no longer touching the ground and screaming, "I'm sorry, I'm sorry, please let me down! Please let me down!"

Ren staring into the doctor's eyes finally snapped back into reality. He released him and

Dr. Taylor fell to the floor. One of the nurses heard the commotion and came running over. "Is everything all right?" She inquired.

Dr. Taylor waived his hand to signify that things were cool. Holding his throat he said to Ren, "I'm sorry Mr. Love. I truly am. I wish there was something I could do for him. But his condition is terminal. All we can do now is to try to make him feel comfortable," Dr. Taylor said taking in deep breaths while making his way back to his feet.

"I'm sorry doc. I didn't mean to hurt you. It's just that my father means so much to me. I'd do anything for him," Ren said as he helped the doctor up and straighten out his suit coat.

"I understand. I lost my father a couple of years ago."

"So how long does he have?"

"Not long. It could be any day now."

With a long face, Ren softly tapped Dr. Taylor on the back as if reassuring him that he was truly sorry for jacking him up. Dr. Taylor gave a sort of fake looking smile as he turned and left. Walking in the room, Ren went over to his father's bed and leaned against it.

"Dad," Ren said rubbing his forearm.

His father's eyes slowly opened. Grinning, he sat up in the bed. It seemed the most simplest of movements required a tremendous effort on his part.

"Hey son," his father said in a scratchy voice.

"How are you feeling old man?"

"Good since they increased my morphine drip," he joked, but Ren was in no laughing mood. "I guess the doctor told you."

Ren shook his head, "I'm sorry dad. I failed you."

"You ain't failed me son. When God calls your number, ain't nothing no one can do about it," his father said grabbing his hand with the little strength he had left. "Just do me a favor? Bring my grandson by to see me. I want to spend some time with him."

"Sure dad. I just have to run by the office to pickup something and I'll bring him right back."

**

Things at The Ship have now hit a new high. Captain Riley officially formed a task force of eight detectives along with several uniform cops headed by McCain and Bernstein to over see the *Hands off Killer* investigation. The Captain even gave them the meeting room for their base of operation. The walls were covered with the pictures of the gruesome crime scenes. Also they had the photos of all the evidence taken like the notes that the killer left as well as the pictures of Greg Stanton and the still unidentified black man that was mysteriously linked to all the women.

McCain enters the room with his normal

stoic look. He sat some files down on the table and gathered all the troops over. Dabbing his forehead with a handkerchief from his suit jacket, he took a deep breath. "I just got finished talking to the Captain. After ripping my ass for no progress, he's given me the okay for more overtime. So I suggest you call your wives and tell them don't wait up for you, because we're going to be working around the clock until this case cracks! Now first things first, Bernstein, do we have anything on Stanton's location?"

"Nothing, it's like the man up and disappeared into thin air," Bernstein replied.

"Okay, Davis, let's run a trace on his credit cards. Maybe he used them in the last twenty-four hours to get a hotel room or something," McCain ordered.

"I'm on it," Davis said picking up one of the several phones that were lined up on the table.

"Barber, have forensics go through Stanton's computer terminal. See what he's got on his hard drive."

"Yes Sir," he answered hopping on a phone as well.

"And Bernstein, we got to find out what in the hell do these numbers mean. 978, 140, 007, 8479 are stuck in my head."

"Well, maybe it's time we should call the FBI again. Now that we have a new set of numbers, they might be able to decipher their meaning," Bernstein added.

As they were discussing that, a rookie uniformed cop came in with the guys lunch orders. He had been given the menial task of going to the nearby Subway and getting everyone on the task force a sandwich. Sitting the heavy box down on the table, he looked over at McCain. "I'm sorry to interrupt Sir, but what were those numbers again?" The young officer inquired.

"Why?" McCain asked.

"Something about them sounds familiar."

"All right, 9781400078479," McCain said running off the numbers quickly.

"I was right, it's the barcode number to a book," the young officer commented.

Everyone stopped what they were doing, turned, and looked at the young cop with their mouths open in amazement. It was silent for a second until McCain finally spoke, "A barcode?"

"Yeah a barcode, you know a UPC number that stores use to scan something that you buy."

"How, ah, how do you know this is a barcode for a book?" McCain asked with a confused look on his face.

"Well ah; I worked my way through college as a librarian. Don't tell anybody that," he joked. "But anyway, I would have to log in and catalog all new books by barcode. And I noticed a strange thing that probably nobody outside the library system knows. And that is that every book's barcode number starts with the same prefix, 978. And the number you said is about the same length as a standard barcode number."

"UNBELIEVEABLE!" McCain stated. "So do you know what book it is?"

"No, but all I need is a few minutes on a computer and I can find out."

"What's your name rookie?" McCain asked.

"Douglas Banks Sir," the young, white, well tanned officer said flashing his pearly white teeth.

"Good job son! As of this moment you're off that shitty detail and I'm putting you on the task force. And your first order of business is to find out the name of that book for me ASAP.

"Yes sir! And thanks for the opportunity Sir," Douglas replied.

Douglas left The Ship and went to the nearby library. His hunch was right. Searching their database with the group of numbers from the *Hands off Killer,* he found the book. Having no library card, he used the excuse of a police emergency to check the book out.

Thirty minutes after leaving, Douglas returned to the meeting room with a book under his arm. McCain and the rest of the officers were still in the process of trying to track down Stanton with no success. He walked up to McCain and Bernstein.

"I was right sir. Those numbers were the barcode to this book," Douglas said handing it to him, "*Love* by Toni Morrison."

"A book called *Love* by Toni Morrison. I don't get it," Bernstein said looking on.

McCain took the book from Douglas and looked over it carefully. The cover had the face of a caramel colored woman wrapped in yellow flowers with the words love written in bold blue letters. He turned it around to the back cover to see the numbers that had been stuck in his head since the first murder. Briefly, he scanned through the synopsis in the back, but nothing jumped out at him immediately.

"Looks like I got some serious reading in front of me," McCain commented as he cracked open the book.

"So you think this book is the smoking gun?" Bernstein asked taking the book from McCain and examining it for himself.

"There's a reason why the killer left these clues. Usually, when killers leave clues they want us to know why they did it. And maybe the answer is in this book," McCain said pointing at the book.

As everyone got back to work, McCain stepped outside in the parking lot to fire up a cigar. He smokes one from time to time to help himself relax and think clearly. Punch is his favorite kind. He doesn't smoke them with regularity because they're too expensive. Cutting off the tip, he strikes a match and twirls the cigar around the flame to light it correctly. As he takes the first taste, he sees a blue Ford Mustang pulling into the parking lot. Getting out the car was Ren. He was wearing his standard gear, a gray t-shirt with a black pair of blue jeans.

McCain watched him close the door of his car and enter the building from a distance. All of sudden a light flipped on in his head, "A book named *Love*," he whispered to himself, "I'll be damn."

He puts out the cigar after only taking a couple of buffs. Going back into the meeting room, he heads right to the wall that has a copy of the sketch drawn by the police artist courtesy of Gale Gordon and snatches it down. Walking over to a file cabinet, he pulls down a large binder. The binder had the photo and profile of every single cop that worked in The Ship. He opened it and found Ren's photo. He put the sketch and the photo side by side and looked at it closely.

"Holy shit!" McCain murmured in a low voice, as he walked over to Bernstein and whispered, "We need to talk in private."

"Okay," Bernstein replied as he followed McCain into the Captain's office. The Captain had left for police headquarters for a meeting.

"Check this out," McCain said putting the binder down on the desk with the two pictures side by side.

Bernstein studied the pictures closely as his eyes widened. "This is our mystery man! Who is he?"

"Detective Lorenzo Love, Love, as in the name of the book that our killer left us clues to find," McCain answered.

"Another detective is mixed up in this? I don't

believe it. There must be some misunderstanding or coincidence or something."

"He drives a blue Mustang, a blue Mustang like the one that Gale Gordon described to us. He looks exactly like the man on the sketch. A list of numbers left by the killer that leads to a book with his name on it. This is no coincidence."

"So what about Stanton? It's pretty suspicious that his wife gets killed and he's no where to be found."

"I know, but he has no ties to the other women. Detective Loves does."

"Yeah, but Love has no apparent ties to Heather Stanton," Bernstein replied.

"We haven't been through all the evidence yet. Who know what forensics will turn up?"

"Okay, let's bring him in and question him."

"Nah, he's got too much pull around this place, especially with the Captain. We need for our evidence to be air tight before we can even think about arresting and questioning him. He's very slick, and if we leave any holes uncovered he'll definitely slide through them."

"So what's the plan?"

"Well, we need to establish a link to Heather Stanton first. Prove that he knew her. And we'll need corroborating evidence in addition to the sketch that shows he knew all of those women," McCain said pacing back and forth and rubbing his chin. "The throw-away cell phone! Remember the clerk from the gas station that the throw-away cell phone was brought at. He identified the man on the sketch as the buyer. If we can link him to the phone, we can link him to all of the women. And I'll bet that Heather Stanton's phone records have calls placed to that number."

"It's not a throw-away cell phone though," Bernstein said while smiling.

"What makes you think that?"

"If you're a married man with women on the side and you don't wanna get found out, you'd need a secret way to keep in touch with your mistress. You know, you don't want the mistress having your home phone number calling your house creating problems. So you keep a phone on the side."

"You sure know a lot about this."

"Well, I'm no saint," Bernstein joked.

"So you're thinking it wasn't a throw-away cell phone, but a permanent phone that he always uses on the side?"

"Exactly!"

"Excuse me Sir, but I think you need to see this," Detective Barber said interrupting their conversation.

"Just a minute," McCain replied.

"I think you better come now. You won't believe what forensics has uncovered," Barber insisted.

McCain and Bernstein followed Barber back into the meeting room. He stood behind a young Chinese man named Lin who was the computer forensics expert for the downtown office. The Captain requested him to be a part of the task force. Instead of sending information downtown to process and having a lot of red tape, it was better if he just worked directly with the task force. Lin stroked some keys on his laptop and turned it around so that the rest of the detectives could see.

"We were able to crack the simple cryptic code that Stanton had on his desktop, and found these pictures."

They were all standing there looking in shock at the photos Stanton had of Ren and his wife making love. The photographs left no doubt that Ren and Heather were having an affair.

"Looks like we've got our connection," Bernstein stated.

McCain stood up straight with his arms folded breathing hard. As much as his mind had locked down on Ren as a suspect, he really didn't want to believe that a fellow officer was a possible serial killer. The whole situation gave him a moment of pause. The wrinkles in his face were more defined than ever. Walking over to a corner by himself, he begins running his fingers through his thin gray hair. Turning back around after a long silence in the room he said, "Okay, we need to call Internal Affair and inform them of the situation. Also we need to get Judge Karr on the phone and have him issue a warrant for

Det. Lorenzo Love's arrest. Shit! Matter of fact I almost forgot, he's here right now!" McCain said as he rushed out the meeting room and into the lobby with the task force following behind him.

They all split up and started searching the area. The Ship was pretty deserted. Since it was Sunday, the place is usually run with a skeleton crew. McCain went into the clubhouse first, but it was completely deserted. Walking over he asked some uniformed officers if they had seen Ren. They all just shrugged their shoulders. Ren was gone.

While McCain was looking for Ren, he hadn't noticed Jason. Jason had smoothly slid into the meeting room undetected and was nosing around. Following Ren's orders, he was making sure that he knew what the task force knew. When everyone rushed out to find Ren he stayed in the meeting room with Barber who was getting the results of the credit card search he ran on Stanton.

"Got a hit!" Barber exclaimed.

"What you got?" Jason inquired walking over.

"The database finally turned up a hit on Stanton's credit card," Barber answered.

"Oh yeah?"

"Yeah, he just charged a room at the Hilton Garden Inn in on Main St. to his card."

"We better move on this. I'll let McCain know. You stay on the computer and see what else you can turn up."

"Okay," Barber replied as his face was buried in his computer screen.

Jason, who had no intention of letting McCain know anything, slipped out the side door and into the parking lot. Quickly, he opened his car door while pulling out his cell phone at the same time. He quickly called Ren.

"Yeah," Ren answered.

"It's Jason. I got good news and bad news."

"Start with the bad first."

"The bad news is they hacked Stanton's desktop sooner than we thought. It's only a matter of time before McCain has a warrant for your arrest. They are looking for you now. The good news, I know where Stanton is."

"Where is that son-of-a-bitch?"

"He's at the Hilton Garden Inn on Main St. I bought you a little time. McCain doesn't know yet. He's more focused on trying to find you."

"Cool! Good looking out."

Ren hung up the phone and turned his attention to Nina. She and Michael were getting ready to go to the hospital to see Ren's father.

"Say baby something just came up with the job," Ren said to Nina.

"What about your dad?" Nina asked.

"Go ahead and take Michael up there to see him. I gotta take care of this now. It's important. It has to do with the *Hands off Killer* case," Ren replied.

"Oh, okay."

"By the way, where is that mini recorder of yours? I'm gonna need it."

"Upstairs! I think it's in my dresser. I'll go get it," Nina said immediately heading to her bedroom. After rambling through her things for a few minutes, she appeared a couple of minutes later with the recorder and handed it to Ren.

"Is there a tape in here?" Ren asked.

"Yes baby."

"Good! Go ahead and take Michael to see his grandpa, and I'll be up there as soon as I'm finished," Ren stated as he kissed Nina on the lips before dashing out the front door.

CHAPTER 23

Stanton woke up with a splitting headache. Slowly, he rolled out of bed and went over to the window to draw the curtains close because the sunlight was hitting him directly in the face. He didn't notice the night before that the hotel room had left them cracked. With his eyes starting to come into focus, he saw that it was three o'clock in the afternoon. The bottle of Jack Daniels he polished off last night had his head thumping. He almost tripped on the empty bottle that was lying on the floor. Stumbling into the bathroom he glanced at himself in the mirror. The stubble on his five o'clock shadow had begun to come in, and now he was in bad need of a shave. Scratching his face he goes to the toilet to take a piss. Only wearing a pair of boxers he lays back down on one of the twin beds and grabbed the remote control to turn on the television. Flipping through the channels he found the local news station. Turning up the sound, he heard the news anchors reporting on the big news story of the day. Another woman was found murdered by the *Hands off Killer*. Then they flashed the picture of his wife Heather on the screen. He sat up in the bed and realized that his phone was still on mute from the night before. After leaving the house he was so mad at her, he didn't want to take any of her calls. He opened up the flip-phone to see that he had about fifty missed calls and his mailbox was full.

In the lobby of the hotel Ren had came through the automated sliding doors. The fresh smell of pine-sol greeted him as he walked through the recently mopped and buffed hall-way. Except for a couple of people reading news papers in the large living room type area that was equipped with a plasma screen television and comfortable looking arm chairs, the lobby was pretty much deserted. He casually walked up to the front counter to find an extremely friendly front desk clerk. "Welcome to the Hilton Garden Inn, how can I help you this afternoon?" She said bubbling with enthusiasm.

Ren pulled out his badge and flashed it to her, "You have a Greg Stanton staying in this hotel. I need to know what room he's in please."

Her smiling face turned serious quickly, "Yes sir," she said swiftly punching the keys on her desktop. "He's on the fourth floor, room 478."

"I'm gonna need the key card to that room," Ren commanded.

She followed his orders without question as she grabbed a plastic key card from the draw and quickly programmed it. "Here you go officer," she said handing it to him.

"If you have any staff on that floor or guests, have them evacuate immediately."

"Yes sir!" She replied grabbing the phone and going through the directory of everyone who had a room on that floor.

Ren made his way to the elevators and up to the fourth floor. Approaching the door with his weapon drawn, he pulled out the key card and slid it into the lock. Cracking the door open, he saw Stanton lying on the bed reaching for his phone. While Stanton flipped opened his phone trying to make a call, Ren slipped into the hotel room undetected.

"Don't move!" Ren ordered in a calm voice.

"What the hell are you doing in my room?" Stanton asked with a puzzled look on his face.

Ren walked up closer and pushed the barrel of his gun against Stanton's forehead. "Why did you do it? Huh? Why did you kill her, you bastard?" Ren barked.

"I didn't kill my wife. I just found out about it. You see I was watching the news," Stanton said with a confused look while pointing to the television.

Completely ignoring that answer, Ren slapped Stanton upside his head with the butt of his gun. "You've had a private investigator following me. How long? Was he in on it too? Did he help you kill the other women?"

"What other women? I have no idea what the hell you're talking about."

"I don't have time for this shit. Handcuff your hands behind you," Ren commanded as he clutched a pair of plastic handcuffs from his belt and tossed them to him. He took the chair sitting at the desk and dragged it into the bathroom. "Sit down!"

Still wearing only his boxer shorts, Stanton handcuffed his own hands behind his back and sat down in the chair facing the bathtub. Ren back peddled to the front door keeping his gun pointed at Stanton while putting the latch on the bolt lock. After securing the door, he walked back over to the tub and began to fill it with cold water. Grabbing the hair dryer off the bathroom counter, he ripped the cord from behind it leaving it plugged into the wall. Separating the lines, he touched them together and got a spark. Reaching into his back pocket he pulled out the small tape recorder. Stanton was now shaking in fear, Ren walked around so that they would be face to face and he forced him to put his bare feet in the water.

"Okay Stanton, we can do this the easy way or the hard way. But one way or another you're gonna give me a full confession of the murders you've committed. And like I said I don't have a lot of time, so we'll have to do this quickly."

"Wait a minute, wait a minute!" Stanton said nervously, "Think about what you're doing.

Think for a second! Why would I kill my own wife in front of my house? That would be stupid."

"You probably did it on purpose to throw the detectives off your trail."

"Please! I'm telling you the truth. I'd never kill my own wife," Stanton pleaded.

"We'll find out," Ren shot back.

He took the wires and touched them against Stanton's chest. He cried out in horrible pain. The electricity flowing through his body caused him to tighten up. His cries of pain were going to go unanswered because nobody was around to hear him. The front desk lady had done what she was told and evacuated the entire fourth floor.

Down in the lobby all the guest were sitting around awaiting word on what was going on. The lady that was working the front desk believing that things were taking too long decided she would call the police. She reached into her desk and pulled out the business card of a detective who was married to the shift supervisor of the property.

"Hello," an operator answered.

"Yes, ah, can I speak to a Detective Barber?"

"Hold please," the operator replied. Some elevator music came on for a second, and then a deep voiced man picked up the phone. "This is Detective Barber."

"Detective, this is Kim from the Hilton

Garden Inn on Main St. The one your wife works at."

"Sure, what can I help you with Kim?"

"I have a situation up here and you're the one cop I know that I can trust."

"What's the problem honey?"

"We had a cop come in here flashing his badge looking for one of our guest. But I think something is wrong because they haven't come down yet."

"Don't worry, it might be personal business."

"I don't think so. The guy was very serious looking, and he told me to evacuate the entire fourth floor."

"Did the cop leave a name?" Barber asked sitting up in his seat. She had his full attention now.

"No! He only showed me his badge."

"Okay, well, what's the name of the guest he was looking for?"

"Just a minute, let me check. His name is Greg Stanton."

"Christ! Okay, I need you to stay calm. I want you to evacuate the whole building now. We're on our way," Barber said hanging up the phone.

"McCain, Bernstein!" Barber yelled at the top of his voice, "Love found Stanton some kind of way. They're at the Hilton on Main St."

Everyone scrambled to their feet immediately. The call interrupted the photo lineup

McCain and Bernstein were doing with the store owner and Gale Gordon, who were at The Ship. Both picked Ren out of a photo array and McCain had just hung up with a judge who granted him an arrest warrant for Ren. After the call, the task force grabbed their suit coats, weapons, and headed for the front door. McCain informed the Watch Commander to send all available units to the scene.

Back in the hotel room, the torture continued. Ren was giving Stanton a steady dose of electrical shock. Stanton screamed at the top of his voice like someone had poured boiling water on him. He fell out of the chair on multiple occasions, and when he did, Ren would sit him back up and put his feet back into the water and continue again.

"Ready to talk?" Ren asked as he took a short break.

"I'm telling you I didn't do anything!" Stanton said in between breaths.

"Okay, let's continue," Ren said, picking up the wires and placing them on his chest once again.

"Wait, wait!" Stanton yelled with his eyes widened as Ren moved closer. "Alright, alright, I'll tell you what you wanna know. Just don't shock me again!"

Ren grabbed his mini tape recorder from the counter and pressed record. "Start from the beginning and speak loud for the recorder," Ren commanded.

Stanton, covered in sweat and nervous as hell, cleared his throat and readjusted himself in his seat. "I killed her. I did it. I killed them all," Stanton said cutting his eyes at Ren.

"Why?"

"What does it matter? I did it!"

"I wanna know everything or we can pick back up where we left off," Ren said picking back up the wires.

"Okay! I was jealous. A few months ago her behavior was suspicious, so I decided to hire a private investigator to follow her. When he gave me pictures of you two having sex, I was livid. She betrayed me."

"Is that why you pushed on the Jones case, to try to get me?"

"Yeah."

Ren stopped the recorder. "You son-of-a-bitch," he said as he clocked Stanton upside the head again with the butt of his gun. "It's because of your punk ass that my friend is dead! I should kill your ass!" He yelled pushing the barrel of his gun against Stanton's head.

"What are you talking about?"

"Keith motherfucker, he's dead!"

"I ah, ah, I'm sorry," Stanton murmured as he looked up at Ren with pleading eyes.

Ren's finger was on the trigger. His body was trembling and his eyes were glazed over. Cocking his gun, he spun Stanton's chair around so he could look him dead in the eyes. Grabbing him by the jaw, Ren pointed his weapon right between his eyes.

"Please, please don't kill me!" Stanton cried out.

"Why? You showed your victims no mercy."

Before Ren could squeeze the trigger, the door came crashing down. "POLICE, DON'T MOVE!" It was the loud voice of McCain leading the charge through the hotel door. The task force wearing bullet proof vest with weapons drawn quickly surround Ren and Stanton. Ren still with his gun pointed at Stanton's head, didn't acknowledge the men as they circled him. He never broke eye contact with Stanton during the commotion.

"Ren, drop the gun!" McCain calmly commanded, as he holstered his weapon while approaching him with his hands up. "C'mon Ren, please put down the gun. Let's try to work this out peacefully."

"This bastard murdered those women and tried to frame me for it. But I got proof. A taped confession," he replied as he pointed out the tape recorder.

"We know, that's why we're here. So please put down your gun, he's not worth it," McCain said softly.

Ren's hand that was holding the weapon slowly started to fall to his side while the others looked on. He exhaled as he let the gun fall to the floor. McCain looked at Bernstein who was standing directly behind Ren and nodded his head. Bernstein pulled out his handcuffs and started placing Ren's hands behind his back.

"What's going on here McCain? What are you doing?" Ren asked with a confused look as his eyes darted back and forth.

"You're under arrest Detective Love," McCain replied.

"For what? I know you're not trippin on this," Ren said referring to the torture scene, "It was the only way I was going to get him to talk."

"No, for the murder of Cynthia Morrow, Tina Gordon, Monique Harris, and Heather Stanton," McCain answered in a cold tone.

Ren let out a slight chuckle, "You gotta be kidding me. Have you heard a word I said? Stanton is the killer. He just confessed to me a few minute ago. I have it on that tape over there. Check it out!"

Ren stared at his mini recorder that was sitting on the bathroom sink. One of the officers reached over, picked it up, and handed it to McCain. Examining it for a second, he hit the rewind button for a few seconds then pressed play. Everyone was standing there in silence with their eyes glued on the mini recorder waiting to hear the so called confession. Nothing but static filled the air.

"Where's the recording at Ren?" McCain asked.

"It should be playing. I don't understand," Ren replied.

McCain opened up the recorder, "Here's the problem, no tape."

"What do you mean no tape? That's impossible! There was definitely a tape in there! He must have found some way to take it out when my back was turned. Search him!" Ren said looking at Stanton.

McCain untied him from the chair and helped him to his feet. He patted him down for the tape thoroughly but found nothing. McCain ordered the men to search the room for the tape. They looked in every little crack and crevasse in the hotel room and turned up nothing.

"Sorry Ren, no tape," McCain informed him.

"What the fuck you mean sorry? That tape is somewhere in this room, you gotta find it!" Ren said as he became belligerent.

"Take him away," McCain commanded.

"It's in here McCain! You gotta find it! Find it!" Ren yelled as they dragged him out the room, down stairs, and to the back of a squad car.

Stanton, still feeling the effects of the pain he went through, put on his shirt and was searching for his shoes and socks. McCain waived the other men out the room as he walked over to Stanton.

"So do you have any idea what Ren was talking about?"

"The man is crazy! He tried to torture me for God sake!" Stanton replied angrily as he cut his eyes at McCain.

"So you didn't confess to him? You didn't take the tape out of his recorder?" McCain continued to inquirer with a hint of skepticism in his voice.

"Of course not! Now if you don't mind, I'm tired of being asked these ridiculous questions. I wanna go see about my wife," Stanton snapped.

"Sure."

CHAPTER 24

Nina was awoken by a phone call at five in the morning. She had fallen asleep on the couch waiting for Ren to come home. He never showed at the hospice to visit his father, and he never called. Nina figured he just got busy with work and so she decided to wait up for him when she dosed off.

"Hello," she said finally answering the phone after it rang half a dozen times.

"Nina, baby, it's me."

"Ren! Where are you?"

"I've been arrested."

"Arrested! Arrested for what? What are you talking about?"

"I'm ah, I'm being charged with murder."

"Murder, I don't understand."

"It's a long story and I don't have much time. I'm going to be arraigned shortly for murder at the Frank Crowley Court building downtown. Come as soon as you can. I'll explain everything to you when you get here."

"Okay!"

"Okay, bye."

Nina made it to the courtroom just as the judge was taking a seat. She made it downtown in record time after dropping off Michael over Natalie's house. She maneuvered her way through the crowd of people that pack the courtroom and made her way to the front bench. No sooner did she sit down, when Ren was being escorted from the holding area by the bailiff. Joining his lawyer they stood in front of the judge as the assistant district attorney began to read the charges against them.

"Docket number 824374 People of Texas versus Lorenzo Love, the charge is four counts of murder in the first degree Your Honor," the district attorney read from his clip board as his eyes jumped back and forth between the judge and Ren.

"Nick Hagen for the defense Your Honor," Ren's lawyer announced stepping forward. "We are appalled at these baseless charges!"

"Save the theatrics counselor. How does your client plead?" The judge asked in a no nonsense tone.

Hagen leaned over and whispered in Ren's ear. He nods his head and finally answers, "Not guilty Your Honor."

"People on bail?" The judge asked.

"People seek remand Your Honor. The defendant is being charged with the premeditated murder of four women," the district attorney answered.

The judge turned toward Ren's lawyer Hagen for his response. "My client is a twenty year veteran of the Dallas Police Force with an impeccable record as a supervising detective. He is a loving father and husband with strong ties to the community. We ask that he be released on his own recognizance."

"The People have evidence that the defendant had extra marital affairs with the victims. He had motive and opportunity to commit these crimes," the district attorney rebutted.

"Their case is purely circumstantial Your Honor. They have no witnesses and no murder weapon. And last time I checked, having an affair is not a crime in this state," Hagen retorted.

"Enough!" The judge proclaimed. "Save it for the trial. Due to the seriousness of this case, I'm ordering the defendant to be held without bail."

The judge pounded his gavel and the courtroom cleared immediately. Nina sat in her seat visibly shaken by what she just heard. It wasn't till Hagen came over and tapped her on the shoulder that she finally broke out of her trance. He hugged her, told her everything was going to be alright, and then led her to the back of the courthouse where Ren was allowed to visit with them before he was processed.

Nina and Hagen walked in to see an extremely agitated Ren pacing back and forth cursing like a sailor under his breath.

"I can't believe this shit! I gotta stay in jail

until the fucking trial! Un-fucking-believable!"
Ren said shaking his head.

"Calm down Ren. Now we knew there was a
possibility this could happen. Don't worry. As
the facts become clearer we can reapply for another bail hearing," Hagen explained with a pat
on the back to reassure him. Hagen took a seat
at the table and opened his briefcase. "I'm going to clear my schedule and work on your case
exclusively."

"Good! And you can start with that son-of-
a-bitch Stanton. 'Cause that motherfucker set
me up man. He's got that confession tape, I
know it."

"I got my best people on it. Let me handle
it," Hagen replied giving Ren some papers to
sign and then putting them back in his briefcase.
"I'll leave you two to talk. I'll be back in the
morning. Try to get some rest Ren."

"I'll rest when you find that tape!"

Nina stood by the window clutching her
purse watching Hagen as he left the room. "Is it
true? Did you murder those women?" She asked
turning to face him for the first time.

Ren took a deep breath and closed his eyes
tightly, "No."

"What about the affairs Ren?"

"Yes."

Nina turned away from Ren and lowered her
head. Ren slowly walked over and gently
grabbed her hand. "Baby I'm sorry. I fucked up.
I know I did. I know I hurt you, and I'll spend

the rest of my life trying to make it up to you. But I did not kill those women. I've been setup. And I need you now more than ever. Please forgive me."

Nina paused for a second. "Do you know what you're asking?"

"Yes, I'm asking that you believe in me despite my faults. I'm asking that you believe in us."

Nina stood silent for a second with her eyes closed. "The vows I took on my wedding day I take very serious. So I'll continue to be there for you. But I'm going to hold you to everything you said."

***

The Lew Sterrett Justice Center where Ren was being housed as an inmate was ice cold on a Monday morning when the buzzer sounded at six thirty. Ren was restless; the light shining in the hallway that never goes out made it hard for him to get any sleep. He hopped up and put on a prison issued jump suit. Normally inmates wear white, but because of the fact that Ren was a policeman, he wore an orange jump suit with the words "SEPERATEE" written in large letters on the pants legs. Plus he had a cell to himself in a segregated unit. These extreme measures were absolutely necessary. If they put him in general population and the other inmates found out he was a cop, they'd kill him.

Standing up in his cell, he turned sideways to stretch. The cell was so small that Ren could touch the palms of his hands against both walls. He pressed his face against the glass door and saw a guard escorting a trustee down the hall. The trustee was pushing a cart full of plastic breakfast trays. They stopped at his door as the guard removed a large key from his hip and opened the tray-lock. Grabbing his tray through the slot he took a seat on his bed and removed the lid. For breakfast this morning was toast, sausage that was tough as rubber, and a large helping of buttered grits. The food was deplorable, but with no other choices, he ate it. Walking over to his combination toilet -sink, he washed his face and hands, and then prepared to shave. He wanted to look as good as possible for his court date. On Friday both the prosecution and defense gave their summations and the judge instructed the jury on their deliberations. And now everyone expected the verdict to come down at any time.

The past eight months, since Ren's arrest, have been rough to say the least. The week after his arrest, his father passed away. Then everything that could go wrong with his case did go wrong. First of all, his lawyers moved for a change of venue because they didn't believe he could get a fair trial in Dallas with all the media coverage, but the judge denied it. Next, the jury makeup, there were too many women on the jury which was bad for Ren. He was being accused of brutally murdering four women; he didn't need women with their emotions judging his case. Finally, all of Ren's friends deserted him like rats leaving a sinking ship. He couldn't get any of his friends to support him as character witnesses during the trial. None of them wanted to be associated with a possible serial killer. Even Dwayne, Manny, and Jason stayed clear of Ren. Captain Riley, Ren's long time mentor, wanted nothing to do with him. The only person that stuck by his side through thick and thin was Nina. Despite the fact of his womanizing she helped him in every way imaginable. Nina helped with his research, brought Michael to see him regularly, and put money on his books so he could buy the things that he needed while being locked up.

Two guards approached Ren's cell and tapped on the glass, "Ready to go?"

Ren looked in the mirror one last time as he patted his hair, "Yeah, here I come," he answered. He walked over to the door, turned around, and stuck his hands through the tray-slot so the guards could cuff him.

The court house was next door, so they walked him through a special underground tunnel for prisoners. Buzzer after buzzer went off as they moved through countless sections of locked doors. Taking him to a holding cell next to the court room, they gave him a nice Italian cut gray suit that Nina left for him to change into. He got dressed and sat on a concrete bench for the next couple of hours when finally a court officer came in and announced that the jury had reached a verdict.

The bailiffs led him into a packed court room. People were lined up against the walls in anticipation. The sound of low whispers filled the large room as Ren entered. Lights were flashing from the cameras, as the media coverage of this trial was the number one story in the nation for the past two weeks. Sitting directly behind the prosecutor were the families of the victims. First there was Gale Gordon; the mother of Tina Gordon who never missed a day of the trial. And every time Ren was brought into the court room she shot him a dirty look. Her eyewitness testimony of seeing Ren with her daughter was damaging. Then there Greg Stanton, his testimony of his wife's affair with Ren was also damaging. Not to mention the fact that Ren tortured him. The defense tried to bring up the fact that he confessed to the crimes, but the judge ruled that the confession was inadmissible since the tape was never found. The other two ladies' parents didn't testify. They were there only to get closure for their respective families.

Ren walked passed them and saw his lawyer who was already sitting at the defense table shuffling through some papers. Nina was standing in the court gallery on the first row. As soon as Ren came over he gave Nina a hug and a kiss.

"You okay baby?" Nina asked while holding his hand.

"I'm fine," he replied.

Michael was standing next to Nina. He was holding his momma's hand tightly. Feeling the eyes of everyone watching him made the little boy uneasy. Ren knelt down so that he could be face to face with his son. Curling his face into a smile, Ren gave him a hug too and said, "Don't worry son. Everything is gonna be alright."

"Daddy, when are you coming home? I miss eating breakfast with you in the morning," Michael asked.

"Soon!" Ren answered rubbing him on the top of his head.

The bailiff stood up and announced in a loud voice, "All rise! Court is now in session, the Honorable Judge Jesse Walker presiding."

Everyone stood as the judge made his way to the bench. The court room fell silent. After allowing the people to be seated, he had the jury brought in. The seven women and five men that made up the jury slowly walked in the jury box single file.

"Has the jury reached a verdict?" The judge asked.

"We have Your Honor," the jury foreman responded as he passed a slip of paper to the officer. He took it to the judge who put on his glasses and casually glanced at the decision like it was a grocery list his wife just gave him.

"Will the defendant please rise," the judge said addressing Ren and his lawyer.

Ren stood up with confidence. Despite all

the set backs in his trial, Ren believed with every fiber of his being that no way the jury was going to find him guilty. He was innocent after all, Right? With a slight grin, he turned and winked at Michael and Nina.

"In count one, murder in the first degree for Heather Stanton, how do you find?" the judge asked the jury foreman.

"We find the defendant guilty your honor," the foreman said staring at the judge, and never looking over at Ren.

Ren just stood there with a strange look of disbelief as each of the verdicts were read back to back sealing his fate. Multiple murder-one convictions in Texas was a guaranteed death sentence, and Ren knew it.

"In count two, murder in the first degree for Monique Harris, how do you find?"

"Guilty!"

"In count three, murder in the first degree for Cynthia Morrow, how do you find?"

"Guilty!"

"And count four, murder in the first degree for Tina Gordon, how do you find?"

"Guilty!"

Ren still had a strange looking smirk on his face as he stared at the men and women in the jury box. His lawyer leaned over and whispered in his ear, "We knew this was a possibility. I'll be working on filing your appeal right away."

Ren nodded in agreement. Hugging Nina and Michael one last time, the officers quickly walked over and escorted him back to the holding cell where he was earlier.

The families of the victims all shed a few tears, especially Gale Gordon, who took the verdict hard. Stanton, who was sitting next to Gale Gordon, ended up consoling her. Putting his arm over her shoulder, he gave her some tissue to wipe her eyes. The rest of the victim's family members came over to the prosecutor one by one, shook his hand, and congratulated him on a job well done.

McCain, who was also sitting in the section along side the victim's families, was the only one who didn't congratulate the prosecutor after the verdict. He just sat there staring at Stanton, watching his every move like a hawk. The Love trial was his final case before he retired. But as he watched Stanton consoling Gale Gordon, he couldn't help but to think, did he get the right man.

CHAPTER 25

Fourteen years has passed since Ren was found guilty. It only took a record ten minutes for the jury to sentence Ren to death. One vote was all that was needed and it only took one minute. The other nine minutes was for walking into the jury room. Ren was promptly sent to the infamous death row in Huntsville TX, the prison that leads the nation in inmates that are put to death every year. Ren's defensive team tried multiple appeals, including federal and the Supreme Court, but they all failed. And so today was the day of his execution.

Ren got up as he normally does over the past fourteen years at seven in the morning. As he rolled out of bed he looked at the front of his cell to see the warden standing there. The warden was this short, fat, pale looking, white man that wore a large cowboy hat and talked in a slow southern-drawl. Slowly making his way to his feet, Ren scratched his balls before walking over to see what the warden wanted.

"Love, as you know today is the day. In an

hour we're going to transfer you to Unit B which is where the execution chamber is. You'll be able to spend time with your family there and have your last meal. Have you decided what you want to do with your personal effects?" The warden asked.

"Yeah, my wife is gonna take them when she comes up here."

"Okay. And have you thought about what you want for your last meal?"

"Yeah, I want a t-bone steak cooked on the grill, medium rare, and some baked potatoes."

"You got it. A priest will be by to see you when you're transferred, and I'll get you the moment your family arrives."

"Thank you warden."

The warden turns and heads back down the hall while two guards stand at the door and wait for Ren as they prepare to escort him to the shower area. Dressed in a pair of prison issued white boxers and rubber flip-flops, he grabbed a towel from the shelf as one of the guards hand-cuffs him. It is prison policy that when a death row inmate leaves their cell, they must be escorted by two guards and have their hands cuffed when being transported to different areas inside the prison. They arrived at the shower room and Ren was taken out of his restraints. The shower was just a long wall with a shower head sticking out every couple of feet. There were no dividers or shower curtains only a hook where you could hang your towel. Grabbing the soap on a rope, he began to bathe as the two guards watch every move he made. This was something that bothered Ren when he first arrived at prison, but now after all these years, being naked with other men watching became a common thing.

After showering, Ren was promptly brought back to his cell where he got dressed, laid down in his bunk, and talked to his neighbor in the next cell over, Jackie. Jackie of course had a death sentence as well. He was a young black man, only twenty three. He murdered a store clerk while robbing a liquor store. Arriving about five years after Ren did, he was only eighteen when he committed his crime. And with their cells being side by side, they naturally became friends.

"So how did you sleep last night?" Jackie asked sticking his little glass mirror out the front of the cell door so he could see any guards coming.

"Eh, all things considered I slept okay. No sense of worrying about something I can't control."

"So it's not bothering you knowing that the end is near? Because it fucks with me every night," Jackie asked.

"I used to be like that when I first got here, but not any more. I made peace with it man. I'm ready," Ren answered.

"You said you're innocent. How can you make peace with that?"

"Eh, I'm innocent of this, but guilty of other

things. What am I going to do?" Ren said as he shrugged his shoulders. "My old man told me there're two ways of dying, on your knees or standing tall. So, if I gotta die, I'm gonna die standing tall. Just like my old man did," Ren replied.

"I feel you. Shit me, they gonna need a whole staff of hacks to get me into that death chamber. Say, can I ask you a favor?"

"Shoot!"

Jackie moved as close as he could to Ren's cell and dropped his voice to a whisper so the guards couldn't hear, "Since, ah, you, ah."

"Don't beat around the bush, just spit it out," Ren interrupted.

"Can I get your collection of Playboy magazines?"

"Sure, I'm not gonna need them anymore," Ren said as he looked to make sure the coast was clear before walking over to the vent, removing it, and pulling out a dozen or so issues of Playboy magazines that were hidden in there.

"Here you go," Ren said stretching his arms through the metal bars and handing the magazines to Jackie.

"Thanks man."

"Don't mention it."

A few minutes later, a team of ten guards carrying shackles walked up to Ren's prison cell along with the warden.

"It's time Ren," the warden said signaling for the guard at the end of the corridor to open his cell. They commenced to secure him with the shackles and led him outside to a van. Sitting in-between two men who were watching his every move, Ren was driven across the large sixteen acre property to unit B. This is the location of the actual death chamber where the lethal injection is administered.

***

Pulling up outside the prison was Nina and Michael. They came to spend one last day with Ren before his execution. Visiting Ren, even for a couple of hours was a long drawn-out process. First of all, it's a four hour drive from Dallas to Huntsville, and that's with no traffic. Next, once you make it to the prison, you're stopped at the front gate for the guards to do a thorough inspection of your vehicle. And when I say thorough, I do mean thorough. They even bring a blood hound out to sniff your car for drugs while another guard is turning the interior of your car inside out. Then you drive to what looks like a rest area where you park your car, go inside, and wait for your name to be called. Once your name is called, you enter through the actual prison gates into an office right underneath the guard tower where a man with a rifle is monitoring everyone who goes in and out of the prison. After that, you get in line for a search. The only thing they allow you to bring in the prison is your keys, ID, and change for the vending machines. You can't even bring in a dollar bill. They're so concerned with visitors trying to smuggle in drugs that they've been forced to resort to these drastic measures. When you get finished there, they buzz you through a gate and you walk through this maze of chain-linked fences until you reach the visiting room. But in Nina and Michael's case, they were escorted by special guards to the prison commissary in unit B where they would serve Ren's last meal.

For fourteen years Nina has went through this same process twice a month to see Ren. She's stuck by him this entire time, always there. Divorce or getting remarried never even entered her mind, despite the fact that she has plenty of options. Although Nina is now fifty two, she has aged gracefully. Not a day goes by that some man, young or old, is not hitting on her. But all her attention over the years was focus on raising Michael and taking care of her household. Since Ren went to prison, she was forced to shoulder the financial and emotional load alone. Michael made it easy on her being a good kid.

Speaking of Michael, he is now a twenty-four year old grown man. He's inherited his father's good looks and charm. Graduating from Morehouse College three years ago with a degree in public relations, Michael chose to move to Atlanta permanently after proposing to his girlfriend who he met in his junior year. It's been tough for him living with the fact that his father is a convicted serial killer and moving out of state kind of helped him get over it. Michael felt ashamed every time he looked into his father's eyes, so as the years went by, he visited less and less.

Michael and Nina were led into the commissary where the warden was waiting. He greeted them and then offered them a seat at a long table covered with a white plastic tablecloth. The steaks and potatoes Ren requested for his last meal were already cooked and placed on the table. The warden had the kitchen fix enough for the entire family. As they took a seat they saw Ren being escorted in by two guards.

"Nina, Michael, you're a sight for sore eyes," Ren said, walking over and first giving his wife the most tender of embraces. As he kissed Nina he turned his attention toward Michael. "I'm so glad you came son," he said almost teary eyed as he pulled Michael close to him and gave him a bear hug. "I have so many things I wanna tell you, and so little time. Here, why don't we sit down and eat first," Ren said as he pulled out the chair for Nina to sit down.

They grabbed some paper plates and plastic silverware and began to fix their food. It was an awkward kind of silence as they all ate their food with the guards looking on in the distance. Ren was the first to finish as he tried to make small talk with Michael. "So your mom tells me that you're engaged," Ren casually mentioned dabbing his mouth with a napkin.

"Ah, yeah," Michael answered looking down

at his plate.

"C'mon, tell me about her? I mean, what she like?"

"Well, she's an exceptional young lady, beautiful, intelligent with a great sense of humor. She graduated from Spellman with a degree in accounting. She comes from a close nit family in Atlanta. She's a couple of years older than me, but we have a lot in common. We both love kids and we want a big family."

"She sounds like a great woman. So have you guys set a date yet?"

"Next summer."

"Wow! That's great news. I only wish I could've met her and been there for your wedding," Ren said in a solemn tone as he paused for a second. "Well, I'll be there. It'll just be in spirit."

"Yeah," Michael mumbled looking down at his plate playing with his food.

"Nina, you mind if I talk to Michael alone for a second?" Ren asked.

"Sure, I'm a walk back down to the vending area and get me a soda," Nina replied as she got up and asked the guard for directions on how to get back to that area.

"Michael, I ah, I don't know where to begin. You know one of the things I miss the most, since I've been in prison, is not being able to share breakfast with my boy."

"Really?"

"Yes. I've always cherished the time we

spent together. Look, I know things have been difficult for you and your mother over the years. And I wanna thank you for standing up and being the man of the house in my absences. You've become a fine young man. I'm proud of you and I love you," Ren said clutching Michael's hand.

"I love you to dad," Michael said fighting back the tears, "Dad, I ah, I'm sorry I haven't been coming around more."

"It's okay. I know why you don't like coming here. Having a father convicted of being a serial killer can't be an easy thing to live with. If I were you, I probably would've done the same thing. But I need you to know. No, I need you to believe that I didn't kill those women. That I'm truly innocent," Ren said looking deep into Michael's eyes searching for some sort of confirmation.

"I believe you dad," Michael replied wiping his eyes with the sleeves of his shirt.

"I'm glad. That means a lot to me son," Ren said as he stood up and gave Michael another hug. "I was lucky to have you for a son. You're one of the few things in my life that turned out right. You're a far better man than I could ever hope to be. Don't let anything change that, you hear me?"

"Yes sir. I don't wanna let you go," Michael said in between sniffles.

"I know, but you have to. I don't have much time left, and I want to say goodbye to your mother too."

Michael let his father go and stepped back. But before he could get out the door, Michael turned around and came running back to Ren to give him one more hug. Nina was standing by the entrance giving the men their last moment together. Once Michael was finally able to tear himself away, she walked over and took a seat. Ren and Nina watched as Michael left down the hallway.

"He's a strong kid, he'll be okay," Ren said grabbing Nina's hands. "How are you holding up?"

"I'll be okay, what about you?" Nina asked.

"I'm just savoring every little moment I get to spend with the both of you. Look, I ah just wanted to tell you how much I really appreciate you standing by me. You're the best thing to ever happen to me, and I'm sorry for everything I've put you through. I love you Nina," Ren said softly holding both her hands.

"I love you too."

"Look, I ah, I know I've told you this before, but I feel the need to tell you again. I've made big mistakes in my life. But I did not kill those women. I really need you to believe that. Even though I've made peace with my execution and I'm ready to die, I am truly innocent."

"I know baby, you don't have to try to convince me. I knew from the start there was no way you could have committed those vicious murders. No way that you were dressed in all black, grabbing those women's hair, and cutting their throats. No way that you could've ever done that," Nina said softly rubbing the side of Ren's face.

"Thanks baby," Ren said breathing a sigh of relief.

The warden came strolling back into the room tapping on his watch as he announced, "Love, your time is up."

"Warden, can I have a couple more minutes to say goodbye to my wife? Please," Ren begged.

"Sure, but make it quick!" The warden emphasized.

Ren turned back toward Nina and hugged her one last time. He held her closely in his arms and squeezed her tightly. They kissed passionately for a few moments as they finally separated. Nina started to turn and walk away when Ren had a strange look on his face. Something she said struck him as being oddly peculiar. Before Nina could walk away from him, Ren reached out and grabbed her hand.

"Wait a minute Nina! How did you know about the killer?"

"Huh?" She answered turning around.

"You said the killer wore all black and pulled the women's hair while cutting their throat. How did you know that? That never came up during the trial," Ren inquired with his head tilted to the side like a confused stray dog.

Nina was silent for a second while she slowly looked up from the ground to lock eyes with

Ren. She reached into her purse and pulled out the missing tape from the mini-recorder and placed it on the table in front of Ren, "I never thought you'd get it. You know it's funny just how small this world is, you never know who you might run into. Take for instance the book club I joined. When I met Cynthia, Tina, Heather, and Monique, I would have never guessed that we all had the same man in common, you. The first book we chose to read was *Love* by Toni Morrison. Sound familiar? When we discussed that book after reading it, we all shared our personal experiences with men. Imagine my surprise when I discovered that all these women were talking about the same man, you. They just didn't know it."

Mystified by Nina's revelation, Ren looked at her in astonishment as he struggled to say, "Tell me you didn't."

"It's amazing that the great Detective Love who solved all these cases, couldn't even find the killer right under his own nose."

"But, but, but why?" Ren stammered out.

"Remember our wedding night. After you made love to me, you held me tenderly in your arms and you whispered something so sweet in my ear. Do you remember what you said?" Nina asked, but Ren just stood there with his mouth hung open completely dumbfounded. "You said that your hands were meant for me, and that they could never love another. That's why I left you the message, *the hands that touch me will never touch another*. You're my man and I'm not sharing you with any other woman!"

"You crazy bitch! I'm going to be executed for some shit that you did!" Ren leaped over the iron table that separated them knocking off the tablecloth and leftover food. Landing on top of her, he wrapped his massive hands around her slender neck and began to squeeze viciously. The guards saw the commotion and rushed over quickly. They pulled out their batons and used them to put Ren in a submission hold. One guard wrapped his baton around his neck; while the other guards used their batons to break Ren's grip on Nina's neck. It took six guards to finally wrestle him a loose from Nina. They hogged tied him by the legs and hands and carried him back to his cell as he continued to scream at the top of his voice, "You crazy bitch!"

Nina sat on the floor coughing trying to catch her breath. Her eyes were still bulging from nearly getting strangled to death.

"Are you okay Mrs.?" One of the officers asked as they helped her to her feet.

"Yeah, I'll be fine," she answered. Standing up, she brushed herself off and knelt down to pickup all the items that fell out of her purse.

The warden had Ren taken to his cell and locked up until it was time for the execution. At ten till midnight the warden along with six of his best guards arrived at Ren's cell to escort him to the death chamber.

"Warden! I'm glad you're back! We have to

call the governor immediately! I know who the killer is! It's my wife," Ren said jumping to his feet with great enthusiasm.

"I'm sorry Love, but it's too late for that. The governor has already denied you clemency. Your death warrant has been signed," the warden said as the guards opened the cell door and grabbed Ren by his arms. Resisting the guards, Ren kept on trying to plead his case while they drug him down the long white corridor. He continued his pleads of innocence into the death chamber as each of the guards grabbed his limbs and forcefully strapped him down on the gurney.

"Wait, wait, I'm innocent! I'm really innocent. My wife, she set me up," he continued to scream.

Soon as they got him secured, the curtains to the death chamber opened up. Sitting there watching was the members of the slain women's families along with some media members. On the very back row was Nina looking on. Michael left and went back to the hotel. He wanted no part of watching his father's execution. When Ren saw Nina sitting there he shot her a cold as winter stare. She just smiled and waved.

"Lorenzo Love, you have been found guilty by a jury of your peers and sentenced to death, do you have any last words?"

"Yeah, I got some last words. To my wife Nina, fuck you bitch!"

The End

LaVergne, TN USA
28 June 2010
187669LV00001B/33/P